Didn't the wish letter from JWC say she could spend it on anything she wanted? What could be more important than finding her birth mother? What could be more important than discovering if she had siblings with compatible bone marrow? Her very *life* could depend on finding these people. Sarah practically jumped up from the sofa. "I've got to go," she said.

D1115176

Other Bantam Starfire Books you will enjoy

THE YEAR WITHOUT MICHAEL by Susan Beth Pfeffer

SAVING LENNY by Margaret Willey

HEARTBEAT by Norma Fox Mazer and Harry Mazer

DESPERATE PURSUIT by Gloria Miklowitz

WAITING FOR THE RAIN by Sheila Gordon

BABY ALICIA IS DYING by Lurlene McDaniel

PLEASE DON'T DIE by Lurlene McDaniel

ALIAS MADAME DOUBTFIRE by Anne Fine

ONE LAST WISH

Lurlene McDaniel

Mother, Help Me Live

BANTAM BOOKS
NEW YORK • TORONTO • LONDON • SYDNEY • AUCKLAND

RL 5, age 10 and up

MOTHER, HELP ME LIVE
A Bantam Book / July 1992

The Starfire logo is a registered trademark of Bantam Books, a division of
Bantam Doubleday Dell Publishing Group, Inc.
Registered in U.S. Patent and Trademark Office and elsewhere.

All rights reserved.
Copyright © 1992 by Lurlene McDaniel.
Cover art copyright © 1992 by Linda Benson.
No part of this book may be reproduced or transmitted
in any form or by any means, electronic or mechanical,
including photocopying, recording, or by any information
storage and retrieval system, without permission in
writing from the publisher.
For information address: Bantam Books.

If you purchased this book without a cover you should be aware
that this book is stolen property. It was reported as "unsold and
destroyed" to the publisher and neither the author nor the
publisher has received any payment for this "stripped book."

ISBN 0-553-29811-9

Published simultaneously in the United States and Canada

Bantam Books are published by Bantam Books, a division of Bantam
Doubleday Dell Publishing Group, Inc. Its trademark, consisting of
the words "Bantam Books" and the portrayal of a rooster, is
Registered in U.S. Patent and Trademark Office and in other coun-
tries. Marca Registrada. Bantam Books, 1540 Broadway, New York,
New York 10036.

PRINTED IN THE UNITED STATES OF AMERICA

RAD   10 9 8 7 6 5

One

SARAH MCGREGGOR SAT cross-legged on the hospital bed, staring at the handful of light brown hair in the palm of her hand. "It's starting all over again, isn't it, Mom?" she asked.

Her mother, a short, plump woman with a sleek cap of black hair, nodded sympathetically. "I'm afraid so, honey. But we both know it's temporary. Hair grows back."

"Sure," Sarah said miserably. "But it wasn't supposed to happen to me again. Not after two years of being well."

"Honey, I'd give anything to make it go away for you. Maybe this time the chemo will knock it out once and for all."

Sarah knew her mother was trying to make her feel better, and give her a ray of hope, but holding the wad of hair—hair she'd lovingly groomed since the last time it fell out from chemotherapy—made hope seem like an illusion. Not since she'd been ten and learned she had leukemia had Sarah felt so hopeless.

She'd endured treatments for three years. At first, the medications had made her deathly ill. Some had felt like fire as they'd dripped into her veins. She'd been sick, had lost all her hair, and had gotten painfully thin, then puffy and fat when her drug protocol had been changed. Yet, her leukemia had responded, and when she'd been thirteen, Dr. Hernandez had taken her off all therapy. "If you continue in remission for five years, Sarah," Dr. Hernandez had said at the time, "I'll consider you cured."

"And if I don't?"

"Let's not borrow trouble. Relapses can be tricky, because obtaining a second remission is much more difficult. For now, you're fine, and we want you to stay that way. Come in for blood work every six months, and as for your everyday life, go have fun."

For two years, she'd been happy and healthy. Then, three weeks ago, her routine blood work had shown abnormalities. Dr. Hernandez had sent her to the hospital and put her back on chemo.

"Dad says he'll bring Tina and Richie when he comes to visit this weekend," Sarah heard her mom say, and suddenly remembered that she was still in the room.

"Good. Don't tell them, but I miss them a lot."

Her mother smiled. "Richie is driving me crazy asking when you're coming home, and Tina's had her suitcase packed since Tuesday, according to your father."

As if it weren't bad enough being hospitalized,

Sarah was also three hundred miles from home. The big Memphis hospital might be one of the foremost cancer treatment centers in the country, but for Sarah, it was too far away from all that was familiar back in Ringgold, Georgia. She looked out the window and saw puffy clouds in a bright blue April sky. She wondered about her friends. She pictured Cammie, Natalie, and JoEllen in the school's cafeteria eating lunch without her.

Ninth grade was supposed to have been *their* year. All of them had made the JV cheerleading squad, which meant that they'd have a good chance of making the varsity squad when they entered high school in the fall. Now, all Sarah had to look forward to was three more weeks of intensive treatment in Memphis and then a new regime of medications and clinic visits for the next few years.

"Is Dad bringing my schoolwork?" Sarah asked. "I'm already behind, and I want to pass. Mom, I can't stand the idea of being held back."

"Don't panic." Her mother patted her arm reassuringly. "Your teachers all understand. What you don't get done before the end of the year, you can finish up over the summer. You're a good enough student that you'll be able to stay with your class. You did before."

"What a way to spend summer vacation," Sarah grumbled. "Why did this have to happen to me? It's not fair."

"None of it's fair, Sarah. But your dad and I never gave up hope of having you, so don't you give up hope now."

Sarah had heard the story a hundred times as she was growing up. Her parents had tried for years to have a baby, and just as they'd given up, Sarah had been born. Two years later, Tina had come along, and nine years after that, Richie. "Once we got the hang of it, there was no stopping us," Dad had often joked.

Sarah rolled her wad of hair into a fuzzy ball. "Would you ask the nurses for some scissors, please," she said. "I'd rather cut it off now than watch it fall out in clumps." She looked at the hair sadly. Somehow, when she'd been ten, it hadn't seemed as horrible. But now that she was fifteen, it felt as if she were losing her best friend.

"Maybe it'll grow some over the summer. I don't want to start high school looking like a freak," Sarah said.

"Honey, you're beautiful with or without hair."

Sarah sniffed. How could her mother think that would comfort her? "Mom, most guys like their girls with all their body parts—including hair."

"If it's going to make such a difference to them, then they can't be worth your time in the first place. Goodness, I hope Richie doesn't grow up to be that shallow."

Sarah bit back a retort. Arguing with her mother wasn't going to make her feel better, and it certainly wasn't going to keep her hair from falling out. "Just ask the nurse for some scissors, all right? And let's get it over with."

Her mother left the room, and Sarah shoved the clump of hair into a paper sack and flung it across the floor.

"You sure got a big room, Sarah." Four-year-old Richie crawled up on Sarah's bed and gave her a wet, sloppy kiss.

Sarah hugged him tightly. "I'd rather be in my room back home. Are you guarding it for me?"

Richie nodded. His fly-away hair was the color of dark chocolate, and his big brown eyes looked solemn. "I put a Keep Out sign on it. I made it myself." He glanced toward Tina, who was touring the room and reading the names on every bouquet of flowers Sarah had been sent. "Tina tried to borrow your green sweater, but I told Dad, and he made her put it back."

Richie's self-satisfied grin made Sarah smile. She remembered when he'd been born. She'd been eleven and had just completed her first year of cancer treatment. Richie had brightened her days. He'd been so adorable, so tiny and sweet with his little button nose and bow-shaped mouth. She and Tina used to fight over who would push him in his stroller.

"You sure got a lot of flowers," Tina remarked, ambling over to the bed.

Sarah didn't like her tone. Did Tina think Sarah had purposely relapsed so that she could collect flower arrangements? "They cheer up the place," Sarah replied.

"Doesn't look too awful to me," Tina countered, peering around. "Private room, your own TV, all this new stuff to read . . ." Tina flipped through a pile of the latest teen magazines their mother had bought. Her parents had gone down to the hospital coffee shop, so the three of them were alone in Sarah's room.

"The days are pretty long and boring," Sarah said. "Not to mention the chemo treatments." She knew Tina didn't understand. Sarah was never sure why she and her sister didn't get along too well. Maybe it was because they were only two years apart, but she always felt as if she and Tina were in some kind of competition.

"I know." Tina shrugged. "I didn't mean to make it sound like you were on vacation. I know this is a real drag."

Sarah felt her attitude toward her sister soften. Tina did have her moments. "How're my friends?"

"People call every night to ask about you. I give them a full report. JoEllen says that she's writing you a long letter with all the latest news." Tina flopped on the bed. "And this is from Scott." Tina handed Sarah an envelope. "He says to tell you that he's hurting in track this year because you're not there to time his workouts."

Sarah smiled as she took the envelope. Scott Michaels had lived next door to her all her life. They'd been friends since their sandbox days and had announced their "engagement" when they'd been three. Of course, then they'd been children, and now Scott dated other girls, but Sarah still felt a deep affection for him. "Tell him I'll write," Sarah said.

"When are you coming home, Sarah?" Richie asked. "I miss you."

"I miss you, too. But I can't come home until they give me a bunch of medicine."

"I don't like it when you're not home."

"I don't like it much, either."

Richie reached up and toyed with the scarf she'd tied around her head to hide her baldness. "Why are you wearing that?"

Tina caught her eye and gave a knowing nod. Of

course, Dad would have told Tina. "I have a new haircut," she explained.

"Can I see?"

"It's real different."

"I want to see."

Sarah slowly untied the scarf and let it slide to her shoulders. Richie's eyes grew wide, and his mouth dropped open. "Where's your hair?"

"The medicine I take makes it fall out."

Richie stared at her head from different angles. "I think I like your old haircut better."

Sarah laughed. "I do, too."

Tina looked self-consciously down at the floor. Sarah realized that Tina felt embarrassed and uncomfortable. It irked Sarah. How could Tina act so childish? Did she think Sarah enjoyed showing off her slick, shorn head?

Richie's face broke out in a sudden grin. "I know!" he exclaimed. "You can be on *Star Trek*. They like bald ladies."

Sarah laughed and hugged him. Tina laughed, too. Richie looked puzzled, trying to figure out what was so funny about his suggestion.

Sarah retied the scarf, glad they were all laughing. It beat crying.

Two

⚬⚬⚬

"**D**ON'T BE NERVOUS. This is only a meeting to discuss our options," Dr. Hernandez began.

Sarah and her parents were sitting in one of the hospital's small consultation rooms with Dr. Hernandez and Dr. Gill, another oncologist. Her father had brought her down from her room in a wheelchair, and despite both doctors' reassuring smiles, Sarah was nervous. She glanced at her parents, who looked worried and uncomfortable, too.

"Sarah, you're almost finished with the induction phase of your treatment," Dr. Hernandez said, her brown eyes serious and compassionate. "Before we put you onto a maintenance protocol and send you home, Dr. Gill and I want to discuss some other possibilities with you."

Sarah had been given a chemo treatment that morning, and she was feeling queasy. Sores had formed in her mouth, and her gums throbbed, but she listened attentively.

"You know, Sarah, forty years ago, most kids with cancer died. Today, we have sixty percent surviving five years and more," Dr. Gill said. "The main reason we don't have a one-hundred-percent cure rate, especially with leukemia, is that no matter what kinds of chemo we throw at a malignancy, some cancerous cells survive. The cancer may stay dormant for years, but eventually it recurs, and even though we might obtain a second and third remission, the time between remissions shortens."

"That doesn't sound hopeful," Sarah's mother declared. "Isn't this therapy going to help Sarah?"

Dr. Hernandez held up her hand. "Please, Mrs. McGreggor. We don't want to alarm you. Yes, she will obtain another remission, but the best way to fight Sarah's type of leukemia is with a bone marrow transplant. Have you ever heard of this?"

Sarah's father said, "Of course, but isn't that risky?"

"It can be, but let me explain." Dr. Hernandez drew shapes on a yellow pad and turned it toward Sarah. "Once transplanted marrow takes a foothold in a leukemia patient, it has a good chance of knocking out leukemic cells and curing the disease. A much better chance than chemo or radiation alone."

"Then why don't I get one of these transplants?" Sarah was eager to learn about anything that might destroy her cancer forever.

"What are the risks?" her father asked.

"We get noncancerous marrow from donors," Dr. Hernandez explained, "and there's very little risk to them. The donor is given a general anesthesia, then we insert a special syringe into the pelvic bone and draw out a cup or so of marrow. Since the donor's healthy, new marrow is manufactured, and except for some achiness in the hips, the donor's up and around in no time."

"But what about me?" Sarah asked.

"The marrow is hung in a bag and dripped into the recipient's veins just like chemo. It migrates to the bone cavities and begins reproducing healthy blood cells."

Sarah pondered the idea while studying the drawings. "So, what's the catch? What's the bad news?"

Both doctors laughed. "You're right, Sarah—that's the good news, a best-case scenario. The bad news is that before the recipient can receive the donor marrow, she has to have all her marrow destroyed. We do that with chemo and radiation."

"Sounds creepy," Sarah said.

"Isn't it dangerous?" Sarah's mother asked.

"The threat of infection is very real and very life-threatening, but we take every precaution. We isolate the potential recipient in a germ-free environment before and after the process and until the new marrow starts growing. We put her on immunosuppressant drugs, which are eventually dispensed with as the healthy marrow takes hold."

"What about rejection?" Sarah's father asked. "I've heard about transplants that don't take because they're rejected by the body."

Dr. Hernandez nodded. "Graft versus host disease is medicine's biggest problem in the area of transplantation."

Sarah thought it was a big problem for her, too.

How could they promise something so wonderful as a cure, then snatch it away with a series of medical enigmas? "So, are you going to transplant my bone marrow or not?" she asked. There was a sour taste in her mouth, and the sores were starting to sting. Her mother poured her a glass of water, and Sarah sipped it slowly.

Dr. Gill thumped on the tabletop with a pencil. "Frankly, we believe that a transplant is necessary for you. We think it's your best chance of winning this battle."

The words hit Sarah hard. This was no scrimmage with a nagging illness she was fighting. This was all-out war, and in order to win, she needed a bone marrow transplant. "How do I get one of these transplants? Can we do it while I'm here now?"

Dr. Hernandez leaned back in her chair and folded her arms. "First, we need to find a suitable donor."

"What we look for in matching donor and recipient is HLA compatibility." Dr. Gill drew busily on the legal pad. "Remember that rejection factor?" Sarah nodded. "Well, we've discovered that if six proteins found on the surface of white blood cells match the proteins of your cells, we have an optimum, six-antigen match. Identical twins have identical HLA."

"But I'm not a twin."

"True, but you have siblings, which increases your chances of an antigen match."

"I could use my sister's or brother's marrow?" Sarah asked.

"What about my wife's or mine?" Sarah's father

blurted out, startling Sarah. He looked disturbed. Her mother looked pale.

"You are long shots," Dr. Gill explained. "You see, each of your children received chromosomes from both of you. That gives them a higher probability of matching Sarah. We can screen them with a simple blood test. I assure you, it only means drawing out a vial of blood from each for testing."

Her parents looked upset, and Sarah sensed something was wrong. Didn't they want Tina and Richie to be checked out? It didn't make sense to her. As a family, they'd fought her cancer for years, and she couldn't imagine having more caring, loving parents than hers. Her nausea was increasing, and a fine film of perspiration had broken out on her face.

Her mother rose to her feet. "I can tell that Sarah's not feeling well. I think I should take her back to her room."

"But, Mom, this is important."

Both doctors stood. "Don't worry, Sarah. You won't be left out of the process. You get some rest, and we'll pick up this discussion later," Dr. Hernandez assured her.

Sarah struggled against her rising nausea, angry that it was affecting her at this moment. "All right . . . later." She noticed that her father didn't stand, nor did he offer to help return her to her room. He looked shaken and grim. The doctors sat back down.

"I'm okay. Really. I'm just sick from the chemo," Sarah said while her mother helped her into bed in her room. "Is everything all right with you and Dad?"

"Things are fine."

The expression on her face told Sarah differently. "Don't you think the transplant is a good idea? It seems all right to me."

"There are a lot of risks."

"But—"

"Sarah, let's not discuss this now, please. You get some rest, and your father and I will be in later."

Sarah was tired and ill, but her mother's distracted, serious expression worried her. Usually, both her parents were eager to discuss any approaches to combat her cancer, but ever since the doctors had mentioned the bone marrow transplant, both of them seemed different.

Sarah told her mother good-bye and watched her hurry from the room. Instinctively, Sarah knew she was returning to the meeting room and a discussion with the doctors Sarah wouldn't be able to hear. She swallowed her fear and fell into an exhausted sleep.

When she awoke hours later, both her parents were in her room with her. Her dad had the TV turned low, and her mother was flipping through a magazine aimlessly. "Hi," Sarah said. Her voice sounded hoarse, and she ached all over.

Her father quickly turned off the TV, and both he and her mother came to her bedside. "We need to talk," he said without preamble.

Her mother gave her a drink of water and helped her sit upright. Sarah fought to clear her groggy brain from sleep. "What's wrong?" She saw them glance at each other. "It's the bone marrow transplant, isn't it?" Sarah asked. "You don't want me to have it, do you?"

"That's not it," her father replied.

Sarah glanced anxiously from face to face. Had

the doctors told them something really serious about her condition? "Please, Mom, Dad, you're scaring me. Am I going to die?" Her heart began to pound.

"Oh, honey, it's nothing like that." Her mother put her arms around Sarah and stroked her lovingly. "But it does involve the bone marrow business and Tina and Richie."

"You don't want them to be my donors?" Sarah pulled away.

"Sarah, we love you so much," her mother said. Tears had formed in her eyes.

Her father stepped forward and took her hand. "Baby, there's no need for Tina or Richie to be typed for compatibility. They're not going to match you."

Sarah stared at them, confused and dumbfounded. "How can you be sure? They're my sister and brother."

Her mother shook her head. Tears trickled down her cheeks. "No, Sarah, they're not. When you were three days old, we adopted you."

Three

SARAH FELT AS if a bomb had exploded. She could not ever remember being taken so completely off guard, not even when she'd first been told she had leukemia. At that time, leukemia meant nothing to her, and besides, her mom and dad had been with her, holding her hand and supporting her. "What did you say?" Sarah asked, assuming she'd heard incorrectly.

"We adopted you, Sarah. It was privately arranged, through an attorney," her father said quietly.

"It was legal," her mother added.

The implication that it might not have been fell like another blow to Sarah. "How can that be? Why?"

"I couldn't have children," her mother explained. "We had tried everything, gone to all kinds of doctors, but I couldn't conceive. The doctors didn't know why, and none of them could help me. I was a medical mystery."

Sarah remembered her mother's being pregnant with Richie; she remembered feeling the baby kick from inside her mom's womb. "How about Tina and Richie? I saw Richie in the hospital right after he was born."

"That's another of those medical mysteries," her father said. "We adopted you, and right after your first birthday, your mom discovered she was pregnant. Sometimes it happens that way. Adoption leads to pregnancy. No one knows why."

"Once we got the hang of it, there was no stopping us." Sarah had heard him say those words many times, but now they took on a whole new meaning. Tina was the breakthrough, not Sarah.

"Sarah, listen to me," her mother said. Sarah turned toward the sound of her voice, feeling like a robot without a will of her own. Her mother's plump face looked sad and tormented. "We have always thought of you as our own, Sarah. I couldn't love you more if you'd come out of my body."

"Except I didn't," Sarah replied. She looked at her father. His brown eyes were misty. "I don't belong to either of you."

"Yes, you do," her father insisted. "You've been ours since you were three days old."

"You mean I was a legal transaction," Sarah said matter-of-factly. "Like when you bought our house." In her mind's eye, Sarah saw her father signing papers and handing them over to a nameless man, who handed a baby over to her mother.

"You were our joy," her mother said fiercely. "We tried for six years to conceive a baby. I thought I would *die* from wanting a baby to hold and love. I couldn't even watch TV commercials with babies in them, because it hurt too bad. It made me want a baby all the more. I got depressed. I couldn't eat or sleep." She looked to her husband.

"We went to adoption agencies, but the wait for a newborn was five years! Then a fellow in my office said he knew a lawyer who arranged adoptions, and the wait wasn't nearly so long," her father explained.

Sarah felt distanced from them, captivated by the story of two people who wanted a baby. She felt as though it wasn't her they were talking about—just some baby somewhere in time. Her mother continued, "We contacted the attorney, and after about six months, he called to say he had a pregnant girl who wanted to put her baby up for adoption. All we had to do was pay her medical expenses."

A pregnant girl. My mother, thought Sarah. She exhaled slowly and glanced from face to face of the two people she'd loved so unconditionally all her life. Dad and Mom. No. Two strangers. "Why didn't you tell me sooner? Why did you wait all these years?"

"It was a condition of the adoption. The birth mother insisted on absolute secrecy."

"Why, was she a criminal or something?"

"We never asked why." Her father brushed over Sarah's sarcasm. "We never met her, of course. The lawyer handled everything, but he let us know that if we broke the trust, we could lose you."

"Did everyone know I was adopted? Grandma McGreggor and Grandma and Papaw Douglas?" Sarah mentioned both sets of grandparents, then realized they weren't her grandparents, either. Not really.

"They swore to keep it a secret, and they have," her mother answered. "As for everybody else, we bought the house and moved to Ringgold when you were a few weeks old, and no one else ever knew."

"My birth certificate . . . I saw it," Sarah announced, recalling the time she'd had to show proof of her age to join a summer softball league.

"You saw an amended copy of the original. It was issued at the time of the adoption," her mother told her. "The original was sealed by the courts. As far as the law is concerned, you are our daughter."

Sarah felt caught in some bizarre nightmare. Maybe she'd wake up and discover that all she was hearing and experiencing was some weird side effect of her chemotherapy. "But the promise you made was for when I was a baby. I'm not a baby now."

Her mother shook her head. "We couldn't take that chance. Besides, then Tina came along, and it was so simple to just keep it to ourselves. It wasn't anybody's business."

"It was *my* business," Sarah exclaimed.

"When you were ten, you got leukemia, Sarah," her father said as if that explanation would appease her. "We couldn't have told you then. It wouldn't have been fair. We were both scared for you. And you were so sick with the treatments and all. We didn't want to add anything more to your suffering."

"And if it weren't for this relapse, for the bone marrow transplant, you would never have told me, would you?" Sarah realized that her voice was quivering and rising in pitch. "I would never have found out if it weren't for this."

Her mother reached for her, but Sarah turned away. "We would have told you when you were older."

"When would I have been old enough? When I graduated from high school? When I started college? You should have told me when I was little." Sarah heard her voice crack and hated being unable to hold back tears. She buried her face in her hands.

"Honey, there was nothing malicious on our part for keeping your adoption a secret," her father said. His voice sounded as if it were coming from a long way off. "We love you, Sarah. We've always loved you. You've been ours for fifteen years, and you'll be ours until we all die. This shouldn't make a difference."

Sarah refused to raise her head. He was wrong. It made a difference. It mattered that all her life she'd been part of a lie. Regardless of its intent, keeping the truth from her was indefensible. "I—I want to be alone," Sarah said. "I want to think about all this."

"We should be with you—" her mother started.

Sarah's head flew up, and she clenched her fists around the bed covers. "Well, I don't want you with me."

She saw her mother step backward, as if she'd been struck. Her father put his arm around her protectively. "Don't speak to your mother that way," he said.

"You just told me she's not my mother. You are not my parents." Sarah knew she sounded hateful and mean, but she couldn't stop herself. She wanted to hurt them the way they had hurt her.

"We *are* your parents, young lady, and I won't have you treating us like garbage."

Sarah recoiled at her father's tone of voice. He'd never spoken to her so harshly before. Her mother pulled him closer to her side. "Patrick, this isn't helping. Sarah needs some space. I understand." She looked at Sarah, her expression wounded. "We'll go down to the coffee shop for a little while and give you some time alone. Tina and Richie will be back from the movie in an hour. We need to decide what to tell them."

Sarah remembered that the social services division of the hospital had organized an outing for the siblings of the patients on the oncology floor. It was part of an overall effort to reach out to what the psychologists called "the forgotten ones"—the healthy family members who often got lost in the shuffle because all attention was focused on the sick child. The mention of Tina and Richie caused Sarah to have a new thought. If her parents weren't really her parents, then Tina and Richie weren't really her sister and brother.

An image of Richie as a baby floated into her memory and caused a cry to escape. Everything was a lie! Her whole life, everything she'd ever believed, was founded on lies. She curled up in a ball and slunk under the covers. She didn't see her parents leave, but sensed she was alone in the room. When she was certain of that, she started to cry. She muffled her sobs with a pillow, not wanting a nurse to hear her and come into the room and ask a lot of questions.

How would she answer them? What would she say to Tina and Richie, to Scott and all her friends back home? Would she tell them at all? Yet, even as she considered the question, she knew she would never be able to keep it a secret. It was too big, too shattering.

Dr. Hernandez's explanation of the bone marrow transplant procedure crept back into her mind. According to the doctor, she needed a transplant from a sibling for optimum success. Now she knew there were no siblings. She was alone. Utterly alone.

Four

PROPPED ON THE tray table that stretched across her bed, Sarah sat and stared at her reflection in a mirror. Chemo had taken its toll on her looks, but that wasn't what she was seeing. She was seeing "eyes of such a pale, clear shade of blue as to resemble light streaming through a window." Scott Michaels had described them that way when she'd been eleven, and it had made her blush. "That was a compliment," he'd added. "I've never seen eyes the color of yours before."

Sarah reached up and tugged off the scarf. When she had hair, it was a peculiar shade of light, golden brown. Her forehead was high and wide, her cheekbones defined, her chin pointed with a cleft. Why had she never before seen that she didn't look like anyone in her family? Everyone had brown eyes except her. Tina and Richie both had their mom's black hair, and although her father was partially bald, his hair was dark brown. How could she have been so blind to the obvious physical differences between her family and herself all these years?

She'd spent the night in a fitful sleep. Her parents had returned to her room last night, but she'd felt stiff and awkward around them. Tina had kept giving her baffled looks and at one point blurted, "So, what's *your* problem?"

"Don't yell at your sister," her mother had told Tina. "Sarah's had a bad day."

"I can speak for myself," Sarah had said testily. Fortunately, they hadn't stayed long. Her anger had burned until Richie had thrown his small arms around her when their father had announced it was time to leave.

"I want to stay with Sarah!" he'd cried, his dark eyes filling with tears.

She'd held him, knowing she couldn't take out her frustrations on Richie. "I'll be out of here soon."

"Don't be a baby," Tina had ordered.

"Stop bickering," her father had snapped. "We have to hit the road tomorrow morning. Sarah will be home in a couple of weeks."

Their mother would stay with Sarah until Dr. Hernandez released her, but suddenly Sarah wished her mother was leaving, too. She didn't want to be around her parents. "Not my parents," Sarah reminded herself. She shoved the mirror aside and hunkered down in the bed.

Dr. Hernandez came into her room, but Sarah ignored her. She didn't feel like socializing. She wanted to fall into a deep sleep, like Rip Van Winkle. And maybe if she woke up in a hundred years, her life would be different.

The doctor pulled a chair alongside of Sarah's bed. "We have to talk, Sarah," she said.

"I don't want to talk." Sarah slid under the bed covers.

"No choice," Dr. Hernandez replied. "I'm going to sit here until you come out from under the covers, even if it takes all day."

Sarah knew she wasn't bluffing. With a sigh, she raised herself up. "What do you want?"

"First, I want to tell you how sorry I am that you learned about your adoption the way you did."

"It isn't your fault."

"And it's not your fault, either. Or your parents'."

Sarah glared at the doctor. "Yes, it is their fault. They should have told me sooner. It wasn't right to hide it from me all this time."

"Most adoptive parents do tell their children. They often start telling them from the time they're very small, but your parents explained their reasons to me. I'm sure they thought they were doing the best thing by not telling you. They can't go back and undo the past."

"Why did you come? To tell me not to be mad? Well, I am mad." Sarah crossed her arms and fought to hold back tears.

"I'm your doctor. And even though you've been hit hard emotionally, it doesn't change the dynamics of your cancer. You still need a bone marrow transplant."

Sarah felt overwhelmed and buried her face in her hands. "I can't think about that now."

"You must, my dear." Silent sobs made Sarah's shoulders heave. Dr. Hernandez gave her a few moments, then handed her some tissue. "Sarah, I'm not trying to ignore your hurt," the doctor said kindly. "I'm not telling you to forget and get on with the program. I care about you, Sarah, and I want to see you well—free of cancer. We have to discuss our next strategy . . . all right?"

Sarah took a deep breath and nodded. "What do you want me to do?"

"Dr. Gill and I had a long talk with your parents yesterday to outline your options."

"You said I needed a sibling to be a donor. Well, I don't have any siblings."

Dr. Hernandez leaned forward in the chair, her dark eyes serious. "I said your *best* chance was with a sibling donor. But it's not your only chance. We can put you and your HLA compatibility factors into the National Marrow Donor Program registry and see if we can locate a match."

"What's this donor registry?"

"It's a nationwide network of transplant and donor centers, linked by computers, that medical professionals use to make genetic matches between donors and recipients for organs and bone marrow. Whenever a person volunteers to be a donor, we enter the blood factors into the system."

"You said someone needed to match me in six ways."

"Very good," the doctor said with a smile. "You were paying close attention yesterday." Her smile faded. "Yes, a six-antigen match is ideal. Research has shown us that with bone marrow, the chance of finding someone outside of your family with compatible HLA is one in twenty-thousand."

Sarah gasped. "What kind of chance is that?"

"Actually, not bad—especially if more people are

willing to become donors. Imagine, if every eligible donor in the United States were entered into the registry, we'd be able to do numerous HLA matches. We'd have a constant source of marrow donors at our disposal if for some reason a patient's family situation didn't work out. Like in your case."

"So, why don't you have it?"

Dr. Hernandez shook her head. "Sadly, we simply don't have enough volunteers. People are pretty good about donating blood, but most don't know about the bone marrow program. Also, marrow donating is a little more complicated and, therefore, more trouble."

"So, I lose. Is that it?"

"Maybe not. We are going to go ahead and start a computer search on your behalf. Who knows— maybe we already have marrow to match yours."

Sarah wasn't very optimistic. "Sure. Maybe."

"We've put up quite a fight against your cancer so far. We can't give up now," Dr. Hernandez insisted. "Don't be discouraged."

"What happens in the meantime?"

"We continue with conventional treatments while looking for a compatible donor."

"Then I can go home?" For the first time, Sarah dreaded the thought. At least, here in the hospital she didn't have to face her friends and the life she'd left back home. What would they think when they found out she was adopted?

"Yes, you can go home. You'll still be taking medications, and you'll have to come back for blood work, but you'll be able to resume a normal life while we hunt for a match."

A normal life. Sarah felt like laughing in the doctor's face. Her life would never be normal again. She shut her eyes.

Dr. Hernandez patted her arm. "Sarah, your parents understand the risks. For your sake, for your health, you all need to pull together."

Sarah forced a tentative smile to assure the doctor she understood. How could they pull as a team when she felt fragmented into a hundred pieces? How?

Sarah woke with a start. Her room was in semi-darkness, and she was alone. She heard the dinner cart rattling down the hospital corridor and realized that she'd slept most of the day. At first, she felt disoriented and confused, but then reality started bombarding her. She remembered Dr. Hernandez's visit. She remembered her mother's coming in and trying to talk to her. She recalled asking her to please go away.

With a groan, Sarah sat up in bed. Her sheets were drenched in perspiration. She needed to ring for a nurse. There was a time when her mother would have changed her sheets and had dinner in the room with her. Sarah guessed her mother was down in the cafeteria. She flipped on the light over her bed and blinked from the glare.

She reached for the buzzer to summon a nurse and saw a long white envelope on her bedside table. She picked it up. Her name was written across it in a beautiful script. She turned the envelope over and discovered it had been sealed with red sealing wax, imprinted with the monogram OLW. "Pretty," Sarah said aloud. "I wonder who . . ." She shrugged her shoulders and broke the seal. After all, it was addressed to her. Sarah reached in and pulled out two sheets of paper. One was a letter. Lifting the pale parchment paper to the lamplight, she began to read.

Five

DEAR SARAH,

You don't know me, but I know about you, and because I do, I want to give you a special gift. Accompanying this letter is a certified check, my gift to you with no strings attached to spend on anything you want. No one knows about this gift except you, and you are free to tell anyone you want.

Who I am isn't really important, only that you and I have much in common. Through no fault of our own, we have endured pain and isolation and have spent many days in a hospital feeling lonely and scared. I hoped for a miracle, but most of all, I hoped for someone to truly understand what I was going through.

I can't make you live longer. I can't stop you from hurting, but I can give you one wish, as someone did for me. My wish helped me find purpose, faith, and courage.

Friendship reaches beyond time, and the true miracle is in giving, not receiving. Use my gift to fulfill your wish.

> Your Forever Friend,
> JWC

Sarah reread the letter. She turned it over. The back was blank. Who in the world could have sent it? She racked her brain to think of anybody she knew with the initials JWC and drew a blank. She had no friend, knew no one, with those initials. "It must be a joke," she told herself.

She fumbled for the second piece of paper, held it up to the light, and saw that it was, indeed, a check. It was made out to her in the amount of one-hundred-thousand dollars! Sarah's eyes grew wide, and she went hot and cold all over. She dug inside the envelope for other clues. She found nothing. She had only the letter and a check from the One Last Wish Foundation. Neither one made sense to her. Who was JWC? Why was this foundation choosing Sarah to receive such a large sum of money?

The letter said it was a gift with no strings and that she was free to spend it on anything she wanted. "Wow ..." Sarah whispered, dumbstruck. "Double wow." Her mind raced over hundreds of things she would like to buy, but nothing seemed important enough for such a generous gift.

"Slow down," she told herself. "No need to rush." The letter didn't put any time restrictions on her spending the money, so if the money really and truly was hers, then she could spend it whenever she felt like it.

With her thoughts spinning, Sarah decided to keep the gift a secret for the time being. She slowly got out of bed and tucked the envelope into an inner side pocket of her tote bag, which she shut securely in the closet. She smiled over the enormousness of her secret. Just knowing she had so much money at her fingertips picked her spirits up considerably. This money would really make a difference. Sarah didn't know how, but she knew most definitely that it would.

Sarah was released when the induction phase of her chemotherapy was completed. During the drive home, Sarah sensed that her mother wanted to discuss all that had happened, but the heavy doses of chemo that had put her into remission had also left her sick and weak, without much energy. Sarah didn't feel like discussing anything.

When they arrived at the house, her father carried her inside. A huge banner was stretched across the living room. It read, "Welcome Home, Sarah!" in letters that sparkled. Streamers and balloons were hung everywhere.

"Do you like it?" Richie asked, pointing to the banner. "I put the glitter on the letters all by myself."

"It's nice. Thank you," Sarah told Richie. She remembered the time she'd returned home after her first hospitalization. She'd hugged all of her family and actually bent down and kissed the floor. Somehow, now the house looked different to her, smaller and less homey.

Up in her room, her father settled her in her bed. She told her family she was tired and asked to be left alone.

"What do you want me to tell your friends?" Tina asked. "They keep calling and want to come over."

"Tell them to give me a few days. I'll let them know when I want visitors."

Tina looked puzzled. She obviously remembered Sarah's previous homecoming, when Sarah had demanded that every friend she had in the world rush right over to see her. "If you say so," Tina said.

"Let's give Sarah some time to settle in," her dad suggested. Minutes later, he cleared everyone out of her room and left, too, closing the door. Sarah lay still, listening to the murmur of voices. She knew that she was hurting her parents by pointedly ignoring them and their efforts to make her feel comfortable. She didn't care. They had hurt her.

There were gardenia bushes planted in front of the house, and a soft April breeze lifted their scent through her open window. From the kitchen below, Sarah caught the aroma of chocolate chip cookies— her favorites—baking in the oven. She also caught the smell of her mother's favorite perfume, and her father's aftershave. She'd grown up with these scents. Once, they had represented security and contentment. Now, they seemed foreign, part of the conspiracy to conceal from her the truth of who she was.

Sarah felt tears fill her eyes. Who *was* she? To whom did she belong? She wadded sheets of tissue in her fists and bit her lip as the sounds and scents of home and family settled around her. A family she'd never really been a child of in the first place.

*   *   *

"Welcome back, Sarah. How're you doing?"

Sarah was sitting in a lawn chair on the wooden deck at the back of her house, thinking of ways to spend a hundred thousand dollars when the sound of Scott's voice startled her from her semidrowsy state. Her eyes popped open. "Scott! I didn't hear you come over."

"When I saw you out here, I hopped the hedge. How's it going for you?" He sat down on the deck next to her chair.

"It's going," she replied without much enthusiasm.

"I was planning to come over last week when you came home, but Tina said you didn't want to have visitors."

"The ban didn't include you," Sarah said. "I should have told her that. Thanks for the cards you sent while I was in the hospital," Sarah told him. "They really perked me up."

He cocked his head. "You look as if you could use a little perk-up right now. What's the matter?"

She told him about needing the bone marrow transplant. She concentrated on the medical particulars, explaining it in as much detail as possible. "They've programmed my information into a computer bank," she said. "If they can match me with a donor, I'll go for it."

"How long will it take to find a donor?"

"They don't know. They search until they find someone." She had purposely left out the part about siblings being the best donors, because she couldn't tell anyone about being adopted. For some reason, she felt ashamed of it.

"When can you come back to school?" he asked.

"In a couple of weeks. As soon as my resistance builds back up."

"Are you telling me everything, Sarah?"

"What do you mean?"

"Look, we've been friends all our lives. You get a funny little expression in your eyes whenever you're fibbing." Scott grinned, and Sarah felt a hot flush sweep over her.

"That's not true," she protested. "I'm not fibbing about any of this. Why would I?"

"I believe you about the transplant, but are you sure there's nothing else going on?"

"Of course not!" It bothered her that he'd picked up on what she was trying to hide.

"This is your 'bestest-ever friend,'" Scott joked, using the words she had used when they'd been three. "And your fiancé," he added. "I know you like a book, and I think you're not telling me everything."

Caught in the web of her confused feelings, Sarah glanced away. "If there is something else, I can't talk about it now."

Scott's smile faded. "Hey, this is serious, isn't it?"

"Yes."

"It's more than the bone marrow transplant, isn't it?"

She nodded.

"You can tell me," he said.

She shook her head. "Not now."

"But you will?"

"Maybe." Sarah felt doubly uncomfortable, not only because she wasn't leveling with Scott, but because she still couldn't put all her emotions into words. "It's hard, Scott. Can you understand?"

He reached out and took her hand. "I know it must be hard enough to think about going through a bone marrow transplant. Whatever else is bothering you must be pretty grim, too, or you'd be able to tell me about it. Listen, I understand. If you feel like talking about it, call me, all right?"

"All right." She watched him stand. He looked lean and tall, hardened from weeks of training for track. "How's Susan?" she asked, mentioning the name of the girl he'd been dating before Sarah had gone off to the hospital.

"We're history," Scott told her with a casual shrug. "There's no one special right now."

"Too bad," Sarah said. But deep down, she wasn't very sorry at all. Not one bit sorry.

Six

SARAH'S MOTHER CAME into her room that afternoon holding a hatbox. "I bought this for you. What do you think?"

Sarah opened the box and removed a Styrofoam wig stand holding a cascade of golden brown hair. The wig was as close to her own hair color as she'd ever seen. "It's nice," Sarah said, but she felt awkward. They hadn't discussed getting it.

"I had it specially made up. I brought them photographs and a sample of your hair I saved from when we cut it. The wig makers are experts. They do a lot of their business with theater people and for cancer patients, too."

"It looks expensive," Sara remarked.

"It doesn't matter. We wanted you to have the best."

The expense part bothered Sarah. She knew her cancer treatments were costly and her father's insurance didn't cover everything. She felt guilty, too, because she knew she had the certified check still hidden away. She could have easily afforded the wig. "You should have asked me before buying it," Sarah said.

"Your father and I wanted to surprise you."

"I'm tired of surprises." Sarah saw her mother flinch and realized that her comment had stung.

Her mother sat down on the edge of Sarah's bed, her expression somber. "We need to talk about your adoption, Sarah."

Sarah recoiled. Talking about it made her feel angry, as if she'd been victimized. "I don't want to."

"You've got to forgive us for not telling you sooner. Your attitude is putting a strain on the rest of the family. Most of all, it's not good for your health to have this thing eating at you."

"I don't have health. I don't have a family. I don't have anything right now."

"Of course you have a family," her mother insisted in a rare display of temper. "We've raised you since you were an infant. You're as much mine as Tina and Richie are."

"No, I'm not! I don't even look like the rest of you. I was just some kid you ordered, *paid* for, and brought home."

"How can you say such a thing? I told you how badly we wanted a baby. You were a blessing, Sarah. You were special, an answer to our prayers."

"Well, I don't feel very special. I feel lied to and cheated."

"We never lied. We simply didn't tell you the whole truth."

"Excuse me. I didn't know there was a difference."
Sarah's tone sounded harsh.

"There's a big difference, Sarah." Her mother
stood abruptly, and Sarah could tell she was quite
upset. "Sometimes, the whole truth hurts. It hurts
because it isn't what we want to hear or need to
hear. Dad and I tried to protect you. Maybe that was
wrong. It's obvious you think so right now. Hurting
you was never our intent. What we did, we did because we loved you. When you feel like discussing it,
let me know." Her mother swept out of the room.

In the silence that followed, Sarah felt pangs of regret. She knew she was being unreasonable and un-
forgiving, but she couldn't seem to help herself. She
wanted her parents to pay for hurting her, for de-
ceiving her. Why couldn't they appreciate the depth
of her hurt? Someone *had* to pay for all the lies.
Sarah started trembling, then she wept.

Sarah returned to school on Monday. She wasn't
feeling recovered from her chemo treatments, but
just sitting around her house and waging a silent
war with her parents was making her feel worse. She
put on plenty of makeup, a new outfit, and the wig.
Except for being thin, she thought she looked fairly
normal.

As she came down the hallway at school, her
friends squealed and ran over to her. "You're back!"
JoEllen cried. "When we talked on the phone last
night, you didn't say you were coming back today."

"I wasn't sure I would feel like it."

"Honestly, I'd have stayed out the rest of the year,
if I were you," Cammie insisted.

"I like school," Sarah said as she fumbled with the combination lock on her locker.

"Only you, Sarah," Natalie joked. "How about lunch today? Can we sit together in the cafeteria, like always?"

"Sure," Sarah replied.

"And how about cheerleading? Are you coming back on the squad?" JoEllen asked.

"I can't handle that much exercise right now. Maybe in another month."

The three girls glanced at each other guiltily, and Sarah realized they were keeping something from her. Was the whole world conspiring against her? "What is it?" she asked. "What's wrong?"

"Um—Miss Connors sort of replaced you," Natalie told her.

"How was I 'sort of' replaced?"

"You shouldn't have found out this way, Sarah." JoEllen gave Natalie a scathing look. "*Some* people have no sensitivity." JoEllen turned to face Sarah squarely. "The truth is, the squad needs six girls to perform the routines. Miss Connors had to choose someone to take your place. I'm sorry."

"You should have told me. Someone should have told me." Sarah could barely contain her anger as she glared at her three friends.

"We just wanted you to get well. We didn't want you to be thinking about something you couldn't change."

JoEllen's words hit Sarah like cold water. *Something she couldn't change.* That was her problem with everything in her life—her leukemia, her adoption, being bumped from the squad. She couldn't change any of it. She had no control over her life, no choices about anything. She felt her anger ebb and depression settle in its place.

"Are you all right?" Cammie asked. "We didn't mean to ruin your day."

Sarah shrugged wearily. "It doesn't matter. I guess Miss Connors had to replace me. I'm really in no shape to do the workouts, and I don't know if I will be before school's out. It's no big deal. Forget it."

JoEllen looked as if she didn't quite believe her. "There's always next year," she offered cheerily.

Sarah could barely bring herself to think about next week, much less next year. "Right." She forced a smile. "I'd better get to homeroom . . . or has Mr. Parker taken me off his permanent rolls, too?"

Natalie giggled nervously. "Of course not, silly. No such luck—all your teachers have saved your place, along with all your work."

Sarah smiled in order to smooth things over, but inside, she felt numb and beyond caring.

Sarah was lying on her bed, staring up at the ceiling, when Tina asked to come in. "What do you want?" Sarah asked.

Tina opened the door a crack. "I want to borrow your green sweater." Without waiting to be invited, she came inside the room.

"I didn't say you could come in," Sarah said crossly.

"Don't have a cow." Tina crossed to Sarah's closet and started digging through it.

"What are you doing?"

"Looking for your sweater."

"You can't barge in here and take my things."

"But I need it for tomorrow. I'm giving a report in government class, and I have to look my best."

Sarah struggled off her bed. "How you look has nothing to do with how you speak."

"But if I feel good because I look good, then I know I'll do better." Tina turned back toward the closet. "Come on—don't be selfish."

Her sister's logic defied her, but Sarah was not in the mood for Tina's antics. "Leave my sweater alone, and please get out of my room."

"Why? Why are you being so mean to me?"

"Just leave, Tina."

Tina crossed her arms and jutted out her lower lip. "What's wrong with you, Sarah? Ever since you came home from the hospital, you've been as mean as a snake."

Sarah leaned into Tina's face. "Snakes bite," she hissed. "Please go away."

"I'm so scared," Tina replied, rolling her eyes. "You know what your problem is? You're mad at me because I'm the only person in this family who doesn't fall all over you. I'm the only one who treats you like a regular person instead of someone who's sick."

Sarah shook her head in exasperation. She didn't want to lose her temper, but Tina was acting like such a brat. "You don't know what you're talking about."

Sarah started to walk away, but Tina grabbed her arm. "Everyone around here treats you as if you're some kind of fragile doll. As if you're going to break or something. Well, I'm sorry you're sick, Sarah, but I'm not one bit sorry I'm well. That's the real reason you don't like me, isn't it? Because I'm healthy and you're not."

Sarah stared at Tina in disbelief. The hateful things she was saying must have been brewing in her for a long time. Sarah felt fury boiling inside her. "Go away."

"I won't. What are you going to do? Go tattle to Mom? Well, I don't care. You're mean and selfish, and I'll tell Mom so to her face. I'm tired of your getting all the special treatment around here. Everybody acts as if I don't exist. As if I don't have feelings, too. I'm sick of it, do you hear? You have no right to be so mean to me. I'm your sister!"

"No, you're not." The words were out of Sarah's mouth before she could stop them.

They halted Tina's tirade cold, and a look of utter confusion crossed her face. "What did you say?"

Sarah clenched her fists and looked Tina straight in the eye. "I said, we're not sisters. I was adopted, Tina. So cheer up—we're not related at all."

Seven

"THAT'S A LIE!" Tina shouted. "Take it back."

"Why should I?" Sarah felt her heart hammering, knowing she couldn't take back what she'd said in anger. She pretended indifference and plunged ahead with her story. "I really am adopted, which explains why you and I have nothing in common. We aren't sisters and never will be. If you don't believe me, just ask Mom."

"What's going on in here?" her mother asked as she barged into the room. "Why is Tina crying?"

Tina flung herself into her mother's arms. "Sarah is being so mean to me. And she's lying, too. She said you adopted her."

Color drained from her mother's face. She glared at Sarah. "Why did you tell her? Your father and I should have been with you when you told her."

"It's my life," Sarah said.

"It's true?" Tina blurted out, pulling away from her mother. "What she said is *true*?"

Sarah was shaken, caught completely off guard by Tina's distress. She'd thought it was something Tina would be glad to know. They'd never been super close, as sisters should be. "Tell her it's true," Sarah insisted.

Their mother lifted Tina's chin and gazed deeply into her tear-stained eyes. "Yes. Sarah was adopted."

Tina gasped, covered her ears, and ran out of the room.

Their mother turned on Sarah. "Now, see what you've done! Why, Sarah? Why couldn't you have waited?"

"Waited until when? Until she was grown?" Sarah was frightened. Everything seemed to be spiraling out of control.

"I'm going to try and calm your sister down," her mom said. "Will you *please* not say anything to Richie. Don't hurt him, too. He's too young to understand."

Her mother left the room, and Sarah felt sick to her stomach. Of course, she wouldn't tell Richie. She hadn't meant to tell Tina, but after weeks of being bottled up inside of her, the awful truth had just spilled out. All at once, Sarah felt as if the walls were closing in on her. Sarah hurried down the stairs and out the front door.

Outside, the night was cool and dark and tinged with the scent of blooming dogwood trees. She stood in the yard, wringing her hands, unsure of what to do, where to go. She saw a light on next door at Scott's and jogged around to the front porch of his house. His family car wasn't in the driveway.

Please be home, Scott, she begged silently. She rang the bell. A minute later, Scott opened the door.

"Hi, Sarah," he said, sounding surprised. He smiled, but the smile faded as he flipped on the porch light and took a good look at her. "What's wrong?"

"Everything's ruined, Scott, and I don't know what to do."

"Tell me what happened," he said, bringing her inside and settling her on his sofa.

Suddenly, Sarah felt foolish and shy. What had possessed her to run next door to Scott's? He must think she's crazy.

"My folks are out," he assured her when she hesitated. "Come on. Tell me. I'd like to help, if I can." The soft light of the lamp behind Scott threw shadows on the wall, and from across the room, the TV flickered. Scott had pushed the mute button on the remote control, and no sound came from the set.

Sarah struggled to put her thoughts and feelings into words. She told him everything, half crying as she spoke. The only thing she held back was about the letter and check, but the burden of them weighed heavily on her. Why hadn't this mysterious JWC considered what effect such a large amount of money might have on someone her age? Didn't JWC realize what a responsibility it was to be a guardian of so much money? To be responsible for doing the right things with it?

"Tina took it hard when you told her you were adopted?" Scott asked once Sarah had completed her story. Sarah nodded, and Scott said, "I'm not surprised. She worships the ground you walk on."

Sarah found that impossible to believe, yet didn't

want to debate it with Scott just then. "I guess I shouldn't have told her," Sarah acknowledged, her voice small and miserable. "What if my parents are so mad at me that they throw me out? How can I make it on my own?"

Scott put his hand on her shoulder. "That's never going to happen. Your folks love you. Still, that's some story, Sarah. What a way to find out you were adopted. No wonder you didn't feel like discussing it with me the other day."

"I didn't know how to tell you. I feel so—so— weird about it. As if my brain might fall out from thinking about it so much."

"It's nothing to be ashamed of. There's this guy on my track team who's adopted, and he's pretty cool about it. He says his parents used to tell him he'd been chosen, and when he was little, he thought they'd gone to the supermarket and picked him out like a head of cabbage."

The image of babies lined up in the produce section of the grocery store made Sarah smile momentarily. "But he's known all his life. I found out just a few weeks ago. How could my parents have lied to me all these years? It's the worst thing that's ever happened to me."

"Was it worse than finding out you had leukemia?"

"In some ways, yes," she replied. "I was younger when leukemia hit me, and it was a shock, but no one ever lied to me about my cancer. From the first, the doctors helped me understand what was happening to me. They'd say, 'Sarah, we're going to draw blood' or 'Sarah, we've got to do a bone marrow aspiration. It may hurt, but you have to lie perfectly still until it's over. Then you can scream all you want.' " Sarah remembered the painful days of treatment, and how her mother had held her hand and whispered words of encouragement throughout the procedures. *She's not my mother*, Sarah reminded herself stubbornly.

"I always thought you were brave," Scott told her. "I admired you."

"You did?"

"I still do. I couldn't believe it when you told me about needing the bone marrow transplant."

"That's another thing," Sarah admitted. "I can't even look to my family to help me with the transplant. My parents lied to me, Scott. My whole, entire life is a big, fat lie. My parents are not my parents, and Tina and Richie aren't my sister and brother."

Scott moved closer to her on the sofa and smiled. She felt herself softening. How was it possible for Scott to make her feel good when minutes before she'd felt so horrible? "I wish I weren't me," she said. "Every time I look in the mirror, I wonder, Who am I? Where did I come from? Why was I given away?"

"Ted, the guy on my track team, says he wonders the same thing, and he's known all his life he was adopted. I guess that part wouldn't be different whether you'd known all along or not."

"The not knowing is getting to me, Scott. I find myself thinking about my mother and wondering who my real parents are, where they are. I wonder if my real mother ever thinks about me."

"Ted wonders the same thing, but he says there's a difference between wanting to know and wanting to search."

"Search?" Sarah asked, suddenly interested in Ted in a new light. "You mean go find his real parents?"

"His birth parents," Scott corrected. "That's the term he uses. He says he's curious, but not enough to hurt his adoptive parents. They've really been good to him, and he doesn't want them to think he's ungrateful."

"It's natural to want to know," Sarah said slowly, turning the matter over in her mind. She identified with Scott's friend, Ted, completely. "There's nothing disloyal in wanting to know."

"Who knows," Scott speculated, "maybe you have blood brothers and sisters somewhere whose bone marrow would match yours."

Sarah bolted upright on the sofa. "Do you suppose Ted could find his birth mother if he really wanted to?"

Scott tipped his head thoughtfully. "In the first place, Ted doesn't want to, but even if he did, it might be tricky."

"Why?"

"Well, you have to figure that if a mother gives up her baby for adoption, she must have some good reasons."

"A person has a right to know where he or she comes from," Sarah argued.

"What if the mother doesn't want to be found?" Scott asked. "Doesn't she have a right to her privacy?"

Not when someone's life depends on finding her, Sarah thought. "Your friend may change his mind someday," Sarah said. "Then you'll feel differently about her right to privacy."

Scott gave her a level look. "I'm not arguing for or

against it. I'm just repeating what he and I've talked about. Don't forget, it might cost a lot of money to dig up the past," Scott added.

Sarah stared at him open-mouthed. "A lot of money?"

"Sure. Everything costs money—not that it should stop a person, but it's a consideration."

Sarah chewed on her bottom lip, her mind racing with possibilities. Why hadn't she thought about this before? She had money now. Plenty of money. Didn't the wish letter from JWC say she could spend it on anything she wanted? What could be more important than finding her birth mother? What could be more important than discovering if she had siblings with compatible bone marrow? Her very *life* could depend on finding these people. Sarah practically jumped up from the sofa. "I've got to go," she said.

Scott stood beside her. "You can stay longer. You can call your mom and tell her you're over here—"

Sarah interrupted him. "I have to talk to my parents right away."

"About searching for your birth mother? I can tell you've decided you have a right to do that," Scott said quietly.

"Why not?" Sarah challenged. "Maybe your friend feels comfortable in his home, but I don't in mine."

She rushed to the door, and he followed. On the front porch, she turned and looked at Scott. "Thank you for telling me what you did. You may have helped me save my life."

As she darted back toward her house, she realized that Scott had asked her to stay longer with him. It made her happy, but now the magnitude of the task that lay ahead of her was all she could think about.

Eight

❧

WHEN SARAH WALKED into the kitchen, her parents were waiting for her. As she came inside, her father rose. "Where were you?"

"Next door, at Scott's," Sarah answered. "I needed to talk to someone."

"Sit down," her father said. "It's past time that *we* talked."

Sarah knew there would be no escaping a confrontation. It didn't matter. She wanted everything out in the open. She sat at the table and thought about the hundreds of meals they'd eaten there as a family. It seemed like only yesterday that Richie's high chair had been in use.

Her father's voice interrupted her thoughts. "First of all, your mother and I are very disappointed in the way you handled telling Tina about your adoption. We agree that she should know, but it was something we should have sat down and discussed as a family."

Sarah felt words of defense rise up in her mouth, but her father cut off her response with a look of warning. "We *are* a family, Sarah. Whether you like it or not right now, we're the only parents you've ever known, and you are our daughter—in both the legal and the moral sense of the word."

"I know finding out the way you did hasn't been easy on you," her mother added. "Sarah, when the doctors told us about the bone marrow transplant, we were heartsick in more ways than one."

"I bet," Sarah challenged.

"We knew we couldn't help you. You can't imagine how we feel. We've raised you, loved you, been through all your medical treatments with you, and now that you need us—need us in a life-and-death matter—we can't help you."

Her mother wiped away a tear that had slid down her cheek. Sarah felt a lump rise in her throat and quickly glanced away. "You are my daughter, Sarah," her mother said. "If you needed a kidney and I could give you one of mine, I would do so in a heartbeat. If my bone marrow, or our father's would work, we'd donate it to you tomorrow. We'd let Tina or Richie do the same without ever thinking twice, if it would help."

"But you can't," Sarah replied dully. "No one here can help me."

Her father came quickly to her side, stooped down, and put his arm around her shoulders. "We can't donate bone marrow, but we can see you through the next few, uncertain months while the hospital searches for a suitable donor. We'll always be here for you, through the good times and the bad."

Her father's gentle touch made Sarah's hostility vanish like water down a drain. The burden of her hurt and anger had grown heavy and made her miserable. Sarah turned her face into her dad's chest and allowed herself to cry. Surrounded by his embrace, she felt comforted, much as she had when she'd been a small child, running to him when she got hurt. After a few moments, she pulled away and looked at him, then turned to her mother. She knew that now was the time to tell them about the One Last Wish letter and check. "I have something to show you both," she said. "It's up in my room. I'll bring it down for you to see."

As she went to her room, she passed Tina's closed door. Sarah hesitated. For a moment, Sarah wanted to go inside and apologize. Tina had thought she had a sister, and now she knew she didn't.

Sarah shook her head, feeling overwhelmed by the complications the truth had brought. She realized that now wasn't the time to talk to Tina. Sarah went to her room, pulled the envelope containing the letter and check out from its hiding place, and went downstairs. She handed it over to her father. "When I was in the hospital, I found this on my bedside table one evening. I don't know who left it, but I think you'd better read it."

Her mother moved her chair next to her dad's. Sarah watched their faces. "Is it for real?" Sarah asked them.

"It looks real," her father said, holding the check up to the light. " 'Richard Holloway, Esq., Administrator,' " he read off the bottom of the check. "Evidently, he's in charge of this foundation, so he should be easy enough to check out. I'll take this to a bank to determine its authenticity. It's a lot of money for a complete stranger to have handed out with no strings," He sounded skeptical.

"Who could have done such a thing?" her mother asked, flabbergasted. "Who's this JWC? Someone at the hospital?"

Sarah shook her head. "Believe me, I've racked my brain trying to figure it out. I don't know—I wondered if it might be my birth mother."

"I don't think so," Sarah's mother said.

"I think we should call Dr. Hernandez and see if she knows anything about this foundation," her father suggested.

A spasm of fear squeezed Sarah's heart. "Can Dr. Hernandez take it away?"

"It's a certified check, made out to you. If it's legitimate, it's yours."

"And if it's not?"

"Then Dr. Hernandez and the hospital administrators need to know that some nut case is running around the hospital handing out bogus checks."

"That would be so cruel," Sarah's mother said. "Why would someone do such a hateful thing to a sick child?"

Could the letter and money be a cruel hoax? Sarah wondered. The letter sounded so sincere. JWC truly seemed to understand what it was like to endure pain and to feel scared and alone.

Please let it be real, she prayed silently. If it was, and the money was truly hers, Sarah knew exactly how she was going to spend it. She needed to feel in control of her life again, and the money was the key to giving her back such control. "Let's call Dr. Hernandez first thing in the morning," Sarah said.

"All right," her father agreed. He stared at the check. "Don't get your hopes up, honey. It looks real, but we must verify it."

Sarah nodded, afraid that her hopes for the money might be in vain. "I'll wait," she promised. An awkward silence fell, and her parents appeared preoccupied. Sarah took a deep breath. "I'm sorry about Tina."

Her mother folded the letter. "She's pretty shaken up."

"I'll go talk to her."

"Take it easy," her father admonished. "We love you both, Sarah. We don't want to see either of you hurt."

Sarah rapped lightly on Tina's door and heard her muffled voice say, "Go away." Sarah ignored the request and entered the room. Tina was lying on her bed amid a heap of stuffed animals and frilly pillows.

"Here. You can borrow this for that speech tomorrow," Sarah said, holding out the green sweater.

"I don't want it. I'm not going to school tomorrow," Tina replied, barely audible.

Sarah found herself feeling sympathetic and exasperated. "Tina, you can't let what's happened affect you so much. It's my problem."

"How can you say that? You've been my sister all my life, and now—and now—" Tina dissolved into another crying jag.

"I can't change it, Tina," Sarah said.

"How will I face everybody?" Tina asked. "All the dumb questions that people will ask?"

"Nobody knows except us," Sarah told her.

"Nobody?" Tina sounded hopeful.

"Scott knows," Sarah answered. "I told him tonight."

"Scott knows?" Tina flopped over on the bed and buried her face in a pillow. "How can I look him in the face?"

For a moment, Sarah was completely mystified by Tina's reaction. Then she reminded herself that Tina was only thirteen. When she'd been thirteen, nothing had been more important to her than what her friends felt and thought about her. But what exactly would her friends think?

Sarah sighed and sat down on Tina's bed. "Scott knows, but he won't say anything to anyone. And neither will I."

"You won't?"

"Why should I? It's nobody's business."

"Not even Cammie, JoEllen, or Natalie?"

Sarah realized that by discussing it with Scott, she'd lost the urge to tell anybody else. Besides, telling it around would simply make people ask a lot of questions she couldn't answer. "Not even them," Sarah declared. "I don't think anyone should know."

Tina rummaged around on the bed until she found a clean tissue. "All right," she agreed, blowing her nose. "If you don't say anything, neither will I. We'll keep it a secret."

Sarah was feeling weak and tired. Tonight had taken much physical stamina, and she still felt sick from the chemo medications. "Wear the sweater," she urged as she stood. "You'll look great. Good-night."

Tina mumbled, "Thanks. Good-night."

Sarah glanced over her shoulder to see Tina sitting in the middle of her bed, clutching the green sweater to her cheek, her eyes red-rimmed and swollen. Tina was the rightful daughter, while she was the daughter of a stranger. Without another word, Sarah left the room.

Nine

SARAH FOUND IT difficult to concentrate in school the next day. All she thought about was the check from the One Last Wish Foundation and whether or not it was for real. Scott cornered her in the hall between classes while students hurried past them. "How are you doing today?"

"I'm all right."

"Tina's acting strange," he commented. "She won't even look at me."

Sarah shook her head. "She has some strange idea that when her friends find out about my being adopted, she'll be ostracized. It's my problem, but she's acting as though it's hers."

"She'll get over it. School will be out in another month, and she'll have the whole summer to deal with her feelings."

Sarah thought about the end of school. As soon as it was out, she would have to return to Memphis for more tests and treatments. If she was lucky, the leukemia would be in remission. She wasn't looking forward to the confinement. "It's going to be a long summer," Sarah said with a sigh.

"Maybe they'll find you a donor," Scott offered.

"They haven't yet."

"Sarah, don't get discouraged."

"I can't help it. Nothing's going right for me. Nothing."

Scott touched her hair, and she drew back. The gesture was harmless and was meant in affection, but Sarah knew that her hair, a wig, was like the rest of her life—an illusion, a facsimile of the real thing. "I've got to go," she told him. Without waiting for a response, Sarah turned and walked swiftly down the hall.

When she arrived home that day and came into the kitchen, Richie was sitting at the table with a plate of cookies and a glass of milk. He was coloring a paper filled with line drawings of tulips. "Hi, Sarah. This is my homework," he said proudly.

Richie attended preschool every morning and was looking forward to what he called "big school" in the fall. He took his schoolwork seriously and showed off every assignment. She had to smile, watching him bend intently over the page, his pudgy fingers wrapped around a crayon. "You're doing a nice job," Sarah observed, peering down at the page. "I don't believe I've ever seen a black tulip."

"Everyone colors them red and yellow," Richie explained. "I want to make mine different."

"They're different, all right." Sarah patted his head and felt a wave of sadness. It was hard to think they weren't related to one another and never had been.

Her mother came into the kitchen and beckoned Sarah to join her in the living room. "I have something to tell you. The letter and the money are on the level," she said once they were alone. "Your father sent a fax of both to Dr. Hernandez this morning. She's called him back and said that there are several philanthropic organizations that do this kind of thing. The chief administrator at the hospital couldn't give details, but the One Last Wish Foundation is legitimate."

Sarah's heart thudded. The hundred thousand dollars was really hers. Her mother's face broke into a smile, and she hugged Sarah. "Honey, this is wonderful. I'm thrilled for you and very grateful to the mysterious JWC. I don't know how this person knows about you, but I'm delighted someone wants to give you so much money. You are special. Do you know what you want to do with it?"

The time had come for Sarah to tell her mother what she planned to use the money for. Sarah knew it was going to upset her, but she was determined. "Maybe we should talk about it after supper, when Dad's here," she said.

"Oh, you can give me a little preview, can't you? Come on, just a hint?"

"I'm sure I'll spend some of it on new clothes."

"Naturally. It's your money." Her mother's brown eyes were bright with anticipation. "But perhaps I could offer some suggestions, what with summer coming up—vacations and all—"

"Mom, I know what I'm going to be spending most of it on." Sarah interrupted her mother's sentence. She looked her directly in the eyes, took a deep breath, and calmly said, "I'm going to use it to find my birth mother."

Sarah's mom's eager smile faded, and her face looked sad. "Your father told me that's what he thought you'd want to do. I said no, you wouldn't. I thought you'd be able to put the adoption behind you. I thought we could do something wonderful as a family."

"It's not just for curiosity, Mom. I need the bone marrow. Maybe there are compatible donors in my other family."

At the words "other family," her mother winced. "I know it needs to be checked out, Sarah. I've been trying to prepare myself for this moment. I didn't do a very good job, did I?"

Sarah had wanted to hurt her mother for lying to her, but now that she was actually confronted by the look of pain on her mother's face, Sarah couldn't stand it. "I'm not trying to hurt you, Mom."

"I know. It would be unbelievably selfish of me if I tried to prevent you from finding your birth mother. Your father and I both realize that your life's at stake and that you have to pursue every available avenue. I guess I've known since that moment in the conference room when Dr. Hernandez explained the necessity of locating a compatible bone marrow donor that we would eventually be facing this moment—searching for your birth mother.

"I hoped and prayed that they would find a donor through the national registry, but that's not happening. I must admit that my hopes for finding an anonymous donor were purely selfish. I thought that if one was found, you wouldn't have any need to look for your birth mother. That's not true, is it?"

"I have to admit, I'm really curious about who she is and where I come from. It's been on my mind a lot since you told me the truth."

Her mother nodded. "Your father and I have discussed this also. We knew we had to help you find her, no matter what."

"The One Last Wish money will make it easier," Sarah said. "At least it won't cost you all anything."

Her mother smiled wistfully. "Oh, Sarah, it will cost us. I assure you, it will cost us plenty emotionally."

"But not in money," she insisted stubbornly.

Her mother turned toward the open window and gazed out. "I must confess, I've always been curious about her, too."

"You have?"

"Certainly. I wanted a baby so badly, and well, if you must know, she didn't want hers at all. I couldn't imagine such a thing."

Sarah felt wounded, thinking that her birth mother wouldn't have wanted her. "How do you know she didn't want me? Maybe it was just impossible for her to keep me."

Her mother turned back around. "The lawyer swore us to secrecy. He made it very clear that the mother wanted nothing to do with her baby. I found it unbelievable, but I was delighted. Deep down, I feared the adoption process, because I thought she might try to come back and claim you someday. I've read about that happening."

Sarah's emotions were in a jumble. How could a mother not want her own baby? She watched her mother carefully, looking for a sign of deception. Maybe she wasn't being totally truthful even now. Of course, for medical reasons, she had to locate her birth mother, but neither of her parents was happy about it. It was in their best interests for Sarah not to like the woman. "She hasn't tried to reclaim me," Sarah pointed out. "Maybe that's just because she doesn't know where to find me."

"I was there, Sarah. You weren't. The lawyer was very explicit."

Sarah refused to accept her mother's story. Even if there were a grain of truth in it, perhaps her birth mother had had a change of heart over the years. Maybe by reuniting now, Sarah would be bringing her happiness. Surely she must have wondered about the baby she gave up for adoption years before. A new thought occurred to Sarah. She asked, "How do we start looking for her? How will we find her?"

"Your father's researching the process. I understand it can be rather involved. The first thing he has to do is try to locate the lawyer who handled the adoption. If necessary, we may have to get a court order to unseal the original birth certificate. It could take some time, so it's a good thing we're still using the donor registry."

Sarah needed a bone marrow transplant, and she didn't have a lot of time. The One Last Wish money could help, but the thing it couldn't buy was time. "I'm scared," Sarah admitted.

Her mom came over and put her arms around her. "That makes two of us," she said. "I'm scared, too."

Ten

HER PARENTS SET up a special savings account for Sarah at the local bank. "It's your money," her father told her. "The letter made it very clear it was to be spent on something you want. Your mother and I feel the same way. Regardless of how the search for your birth mother turns out, I can't imagine it's costing the full hundred thousand. You should have plenty left over for college, or for anything else you might want to do."

No one said a word about the worst-case scenario, what Sarah knew was in their minds: If they couldn't find a bone marrow donor, there would be no college, no *life* for Sarah. She forced herself not to think about that possibility and concentrated on the last weeks of school and on her hopes of finding her birth mother.

Sarah's father was trying to locate the attorney who had handled her adoption; the lawyer, they'd learned, had retired and moved to Florida. "I'm hoping that once I reach him, he'll give us the woman's name without our having to go through the courts," he explained to Sarah.

"Her name?" Sarah asked.

"Obviously, we need her name before we can begin to search for her. The lawyer, Mr. Dodkin, knows her name, but he's under no obligation to divulge it without a court order. He can also help get a copy of your original birth certificate, which contains her name.

"There's an organization called Independent Search Consultants, and I've learned a lot from them. They are trained professionals who help adoptees find their birth parents. One of the women there, Mrs. Kolelin, has been very helpful. She told me that once we get your birth mother's name, we can begin the search in earnest. It won't be easy. No telling what's happened to her over the years or where she might be living."

"Can these people help us?" Sarah asked, eager for the search to start.

"There are records searchers, who tell me that no matter how obscure the trail is, there's always a clue in the paperwork left behind—physicians' records, social security registrations, tax records, information like that. Once we have a name, we hire a private investigator, one who's handled cases like this before, and the PI will find a current address on her."

"What if the lawyer won't tell us her name?" she asked. The entire situation felt like a TV movie, from the One Last Wish Foundation's mysterious check to hiring a private detective. She didn't say anything to her father and just kept listening.

"Fortunately, in Arkansas, the courts are fairly lenient about opening records for medical reasons."

"Why Arkansas when we live in Georgia?" Sarah asked, confused.

"That's where you were born, Sarah—in Little Rock, Arkansas."

It took Sarah days to adjust to the information that she hadn't been born in Georgia. All her life, she'd believed she had been born in Ringgold, at the same hospital as Tina and Richie. Now, she discovered another lie that had been fabricated to "protect her."

"What're you doing?" JoEllen asked when she found Sarah in the library one day after school.

"A report," Sarah fibbed.

"About what?"

"Arkansas."

JoEllen made a face. "Don't you ever quit? School's out in two weeks. Why work so hard now?"

"It's personal. It's a report just for me."

"Tell me what it's about." JoEllen's interest was real.

Sarah was tempted to spill all. Keeping her past a secret was taking its toll on her, but she remembered her promise to Tina. It still mattered to Tina that kids not know that she and Sarah weren't blood sisters. Sarah flipped the encyclopedia shut and turned to JoEllen. "Actually, it's for extra credit. I missed so many tests when I was hospitalized."

"Is that all?" JoEllen looked disappointed.

"That's all," Sarah replied, flashing a bright smile to discourage any further questions.

* * *

On Memorial Day, Scott's family hosted the neighborhood's annual picnic and barbecue. Every family on the block showed up and brought a dish to share. By late afternoon, both Scott's and Sarah's yards were overrun with people. The aroma of sizzling hamburgers and hot dogs saturated the air, and music blasted from outdoor speakers.

Sarah heaped her plate with food from a picnic table and made her way to the back corner of her yard. She ducked a flying Frisbee and slipped through a break in the hedge to a small clearing sheltered by a canopy of leaves. This spot had served as a hideaway she'd shared with Tina when they'd been younger. The ground was bare dirt except for two weathered tree stumps. Sarah sat on one of the stumps, balancing her paper plate on her knees.

"Are you in there, Sarah?" Scott's head poked through the hole in the hedge. "I thought I saw you sneak back here," he said with an easy grin.

"Too much racket out there. I wanted to eat in peace and quiet," Sarah explained.

"Want some company?"

"Sure. Pull up a stump."

Juggling a plate and a large slice of watermelon, he settled on the other stump. "I'd forgotten about this place," he remarked. "I haven't been back here in ages."

"I was just thinking about the tea parties Tina and I used to give for our dolls. We sat the dolls in circles around these stumps and served them tap water and cookies."

Scott smiled impishly. "I remember the talent show you gave for your teddy bears, too."

"You saw that?" Sarah gasped. Tina and she had

been six and eight years old, respectively, when they'd put on that particular show in the clearing. "We thought no one knew about it."

"I crawled on my stomach and peeked through the hedge. You did a tap dance, and Tina sang a song."

Sarah laughed as the memory flowed over her. "Weren't we awful!"

"I thought you were very talented. And the teddy bears didn't seem to object."

"They had no choice. I told them no supper if they weren't a good audience."

"Isn't this where I proposed to you?" Scott asked, glancing around the clearing.

How could Sarah forget that day? He'd given her a ring from a box of Cracker Jack and kissed her. It had been her first kiss, even though it wasn't a serious one. "We were just kids," she said. "That seems as if it happened a million years ago."

Sitting in the twilight with Scott, with the sounds of laughing children coming from the far side of the hedge, Sarah felt an eerie sadness creep over her as her childhood memories returned. "Sometimes, I wish I could go back in time and be a kid again—to the time before I got leukemia, when my life wasn't so complicated."

"Any news on your search?" he asked.

"Nothing yet. I really hope we find her soon."

"Because of the bone marrow?"

"Not only that. I want to meet her. I want to see somebody who looks like me. Did you know I was born in Arkansas? I've been reading everything I can about that state."

"Why? What difference does it make where you were born?"

"Don't you see? Everything I've been told about myself hasn't been true. I'm not really a McGreggor. All the things I believed to be true, all the people I've ever thought were 'mine,' really aren't. Somewhere out there—" Sarah gestured, "is my real family, whose blood and genes have been passed along to me. I don't know them, but I want to know them.

"I went to the library to read about Arkansas. I felt more connected knowing about that place. I felt like, 'Here's the place where the real Sarah comes from.' I want to know all about it, because it helps me know a little more about *me*." Sarah glanced over at Scott. Shadows covered his face. "I'm talking too much and not making any sense—sorry," she said with a shake of her head.

"Ted, the guy on the track team, wonders about those things, too."

"He does?"

"He says that when he gets ticked off at his parents, he imagines his real ones. They wouldn't hassle him. They'd be understanding. They'd be perfect." Scott chuckled. "I tell him, 'Get serious. All parents hassle their kids. It's their role in life.'"

"Does he believe you?"

"Sure." Scott's voice came out of the dark. "He knows that these fantasy people, these perfect parents, are all in his imagination. He knows that some kids pretend they were adopted when they are mad at their parents. Nobody's perfect, for sure."

Sarah felt a twinge of guilt. She had spent hours imagining what her birth mother could be like. Sarah hoped she was pretty. Maybe even rich. Or famous. "I guess imaginations have a way of taking over," Sarah admitted. "In a way, that's what makes me all the more anxious to meet my real mother. Then, I'll know for certain what she's like, and I won't have to make up things anymore."

From the far side of the hedge, Sarah heard her mom calling her name. "I guess we'd better get back before they send out a posse."

Scott tossed the rind of his melon into the darkness, wiped his hands on his jeans, and helped Sarah to her feet. She was close enough to feel his breath on her cheek. She wondered what it would be like to have him kiss her again. This time, for real.

"Sarah," he said, "don't get all your hopes pinned on your birth mother."

"What do you mean?" In the darkness, his presence felt warm and comforting.

"Sometimes, *wondering* about something is a whole lot more exciting than *knowing* about it."

She thought about what he'd said. "It isn't excitement that I'm after, Scott. It's truth. Don't you see? No matter what the truth is, it's better than lies or fantasy."

"I hope you're right. I hope your birth mother is worth the effort to find her. After all, both financially and emotionally—for you and everyone— this is going to cost a lot." Scott edged closer and lifted her chin. But the spell was broken when she heard Richie calling, "Sarah! Where are you, Sarah?"

Scott sighed. "Come on, my dad's made his own ice cream. I'll grab us a dish."

She followed him through the hole in the hedge.

She almost couldn't bear to fantasize about what might happen with Scott. He was not the usual guy; she knew that. He wasn't afraid of her because she had cancer. He wasn't turned off because she had problems. Maybe her luck was changing.

Eleven

~~~

Two days after school ended, Sarah returned to the hospital in Memphis. Dr. Hernandez began new treatments. A Broviac catheter was inserted into a vein in Sarah's chest. The semipermanent plastic tubing made it possible for her to receive her chemo without having to be constantly stuck with needles. Sarah knew it was better than having her veins collapsing from constant jabbing, but she disliked the catheter. It required constant care so that the site didn't get infected. When she finally could go home, she wouldn't be able to go swimming all summer.

Dr. Hernandez listened thoughtfully as Sarah confided about searching for her birth mother. "The best we could get with blood siblings or even your natural mother would be a two-antigen match," the doctor explained.

"That's better than nothing, isn't it?" Sarah asked.

"I'd settle for it. Perhaps your birth mother might

know the whereabouts of your natural father—he and any children he might have fathered are also potential donors, you know."

Although Sarah had wondered about the identity of her father since she'd learned of her adoption, he seemed far more inaccessible than her birth mother. After all, the lawyer had informed Sarah's parents that she'd been born out of wedlock. And, Sarah reasoned, if her natural parents had married, she would never have been given up for adoption. "First, we have to find *her*," Sarah said.

"The sooner, the better," Dr. Hernandez said as she left the room.

Sarah's mother did not stay with her at the hospital in Memphis. "With no school for Tina and Richie, and with your father's work schedule, I have to be at home," her mom had explained. "Will you be all right without me? We'll drive up for the weekend."

"I'm fifteen, Mom. Of course I'll be all right," Sarah had assured her mother in a firm tone of voice. Now, Sarah missed her presence and companionship. The nights in the hospital seemed endless.

Sometimes, she pulled out the incredible letter and read it for the millionth time. She had brought it with her because she found the now familiar words comforting. She longed to talk to JWC face-to-face and had half hoped that while she was in the hospital, JWC might attempt to meet with her. She knew that JWC wasn't her mother; she only wished she knew who it was. "My wish helped me find purpose, faith, and courage." The words of the letter echoed in her mind. Sarah longed for courage to face what lay ahead of her.

When her family came that weekend, Sarah sat with Richie while her parents were talking to the doctors and Tina had gone for some snacks. "What're you doing this summer?" she asked him.

"Playing," he said, then added, "I miss you. Aren't you ever going to get well, Sarah?"

His question tugged at her heart. "I'm trying to," she told him. "It's hard."

"I don't like cancer. When I say my prayers at night, I ask God to make it go away from you."

Sarah pulled Richie closer and kissed his cheek. "Thank you, Richie. I pray for the same thing."

"When I grow up, I'll be a doctor and help all the people who have cancer. If you're not all better by then, I'll help you, too. You can live with me, and I'll take care of you."

His innocence brought a lump to her throat. "I think you'll be a great doctor. You grow up and be the best doctor in the world, all right?"

"All right. I'll do it for you, Sarah." His small face broke into a grin. "Guess what? I have a secret club-house in our backyard."

"You do? Where?"

He peeked around the empty room, leaned closer, and whispered, "Through a hole in the hedge. Now you know, too, but don't tell," Richie begged. "When you come home, I'll show it to you. It's a secret, okay?"

"Our secret," Sarah assured him, glad that Richie had found what she hadn't had time to show him.

"I learned a new song. Want to hear it?" Sarah nodded, and he began to sing in a high, warbling voice. Just as he finished, Tina swooped into the room, carrying treats.

"I bought you some ice cream, Richie, but you have to eat it over there." She pointed to a small table in front of a TV set.

"I want to stay here with Sarah," he said, jutting his lower lip.

"You know the rules," Tina insisted in her bossiest voice. "No eating on sofas. Besides, it's my turn to talk to Sarah. Don't hog her."

Sarah was surprised by Tina's wanting to talk to her alone. The ice cream was an obvious ploy to remove Richie from earshot. "Go on," Sarah urged him. "Eat it before it melts. You can come sit with me once you're finished."

Richie carried the bag to the table. Tina turned on the TV for him, then returned and flopped down next to Sarah. "What's up?" Sarah asked.

"Dad and Mom are helping you look for your other mother, aren't they? I can't believe you're really trying to find her."

Tina's accusatory, angry tone caught Sarah off guard. "So, what if I am?"

"I don't think it's very nice of you, that's all."

"Not *nice* of me? What's that supposed to mean?"

"Well, they've been your parents all your life, and now you're treating them as if their feelings don't matter. I know you're making them help you look for her."

Sarah got angry. "You don't know what you're talking about. Mom and Dad are helping me because they want to, not because I'm making them."

"You're not at home now, Sarah, so you don't

know, but I see Mom crying, and I know it's because she thinks you're trying to trade her in."

Flabbergasted, Sarah stared at Tina. "You're wrong," Sara declared, trying to register Tina's words. "If she cries, it's because I have cancer."

"And that's another thing—this bone marrow transplant."

"You know I need compatible bone marrow," Sarah blurted out. "I might have brothers and sisters somewhere who can help me."

"What about me?" Two bright spots of color had appeared on Tina's cheeks.

"What about you?"

"How come you never asked me for my bone marrow?"

"Because we're not compatible." Sarah felt exasperated and confused. Why was Tina behaving like this? Mom and Dad had explained the medical facts to her.

"How do you know we're not? Nobody ever checked me."

"I'm sure we're not."

"But how do you *know*?" Tina's voice wavered, and Sarah saw hurt in her eyes.

"Since we don't have the same parents, it isn't likely that you are," she explained patiently, suddenly aware that Tina cared.

"Everybody in this family treats me like a baby or worse, like I'm nonexistent. Nobody takes into account *my* feelings."

"No one meant to—"

"I should be tested. Maybe we are compatible and just don't know it. And how will we ever know if I'm not tested?"

Seeing how passionate Tina felt about being tested upset Sarah. "Nobody meant to ignore you, Tina. I guess since medically you're not a match, we didn't ask you to be tested. I never thought you might want to be tested."

"Why shouldn't I? I know we're not really blood sisters, but I'm a person close to you, and I'd like to help."

"It's great of you to want to be tested, Tina. I appreciate it." Sara felt overwhelmed by her sister's offer. "We'll talk to Mom and Dad about it, and they can ask Dr. Hernandez."

Tina sat back on the couch, looking mollified. "Sometimes, answers are right in your own backyard," she said.

Sarah caught the subtle message: So, why go looking for them elsewhere? It hadn't occurred to her that the search for her birth mother would be so troubling for Tina. *Why was it Tina's problem*, she wondered.

By the middle of the week, Sarah was totally bored. She was the only teenager on the floor undergoing treatment, so she visited the younger patients and played games with them. But she still wished for something else to do.

One afternoon, her father arrived unexpectedly. "Dad, you aren't supposed to be here until the weekend. Is anything wrong?"

"Everything's fine," he answered quietly. "I have business here in Memphis, and I have some news that couldn't wait."

Sarah's heart raced. "What?"

"The lawyer came through for us, honey. It seems

he has a granddaughter about your age, and he was sympathetic when I told him about your condition. He went through his files and sent me a copy of your surrender agreement."

"What's that?"

Her father was smiling, looking excited and boyish. "It's the legal paper your natural mother signed when she gave you up for adoption."

Sarah's mouth went dry, and for a moment she was afraid she might throw up, not from her medications, but from tension. "So, what does that mean?"

"It means we have a name. We have *her* name."

Twelve

SARAH'S FATHER HELPED her into bed, reached into the inside pocket of his coat jacket, and pulled out a sheet of white paper.

Her fingers trembled as she took it. She was almost afraid to open it, overwhelmed by the knowledge that the mysterious woman who had borne her was about to take on a name.

"Go on, honey," her dad said. "It's all right. This is what we've been waiting for so we can find a donor."

Sarah unfolded the paper. It was typed and looked neat and formal. At the top were the words "Agreement for the Surrender of My Child for Adoption." The first sentence began, "I, Janelle Warren . . ." Her gaze flew up to her father's. "Janelle's a pretty name, isn't it?"

"Yes," he agreed.

Sarah read further, ". . . being the mother of a female child named (Baby Girl) Warren . . ." She stopped reading. Was that all Sarah had been to her—Baby Girl Warren? Hadn't Janelle even bothered to give her baby a name? Sarah's vision blurred, but she continued to read, ". . . and having sole right to custody and control of said child, said child having been born out of wedlock . . ."

Sarah winced. Of course, she'd known for some time that her natural mother and father had never married, but seeing the words in black and white cut through her like a knife. The remainder of the document was full of dates and places and legal phrases about relinquishing all rights to "said child."

At the bottom, Janelle Warren had signed her name. Sarah studied the signature. The writing was small and neat, as orderly as the document giving her up for adoption. She ran her fingertips over the black letters, as if the act of touching them might bring the person of Janelle Warren closer to her.

"Are you all right?" her father asked.

"Sure," Sarah answered with a shrug. "It's just weird, that's all."

"It's weird for me, too," he told her. "I never thought we'd have to go back to the past in order to give you a future."

Sarah knew she should be happy about the discovery, and in a way, she was. She now knew her birth mother's name. They'd moved closer toward her ultimate goal of finding her. Still, it was scary for Sarah. She'd taken a first step down what seemed an endless road, and good or bad, there would be no turning back.

*   *   *

Sarah returned home ill and demoralized. Every period of intensive chemo left her sicker and weaker, and each recovery period was more difficult and took longer. She struggled to overcome the side effects, wanting to be ready to meet her birth mother if the records searcher was able to turn up anything. When she was strong enough, her father brought her and her mom to his office downtown. "I want you to meet the detective we've hired," her father said.

Sarah felt fidgety. Her mom obviously was upset. Tina had been right about that much. Sitting in her dad's sun-warmed office and watching her mother toy nervously with her rings made Sarah feel sorry for her parents. Yet, they had been the ones to keep the truth from her all these years. She hadn't asked to be born, or adopted, or lied to, and she certainly had never asked to be stricken with leukemia.

Her dad brought in a man, who smiled and offered Sarah his hand. "Hi. I'm Mike Lions," he said. He was a short, slim man with thinning hair, glasses, and a quiet voice. Sarah's surprise must have shown on her face, because Mike said, "I know I don't fulfill most people's expectations about PIs, but all those macho types on TV and in the movies give hardworking, ordinary guys like me a false image." He grinned. "So, I don't look like a movie star private eye. I've learned to live with it. I assure you, I'm very good at what I do in spite of it."

Sarah flushed and returned his smile. "I need to find my birth mother," she told him.

"Your father's told me. And he's told me about your special circumstances," Mike replied. "Therefore, your case gets top priority. While I can't promise you that I'll find her, I will tell you this—if I can't, no one else can, either."

His confidence in his ability made Sarah feel confident, too. He acted as if he understood the urgency of her search. "What do I do now?" Sarah asked.

"You wait to hear from me."

It seemed too simple. Sarah was still curious. "Once you find her, what happens?"

Mike's expression grew serious. "I want to be honest with you and your folks, Sarah. Birth parents don't always want to be found. If that's the case, when they are located, they can panic."

Sarah saw her mom shift forward in her chair. Hadn't she been telling Sarah the same thing all along? Sarah hated giving her the satisfaction of thinking she was correct.

"How do they panic?" Mrs. McGreggor asked. "Sarah won't be in any danger, will she?"

"Of course not," Mike assured her. "Once I find the natural mother, I use caution in establishing actual contact. Usually, I approach the subject on the phone. I say something like, 'Someone wants to meet you who was born on—,' and I give the searcher's birth date. Believe me, that special date is engraved in the birth mother's memory forever. No one ever forgets it."

"It must come as quite a shock," Sarah's dad said.

"Yes, it usually does. Some birth parents are overjoyed. They've wondered for years about the baby they gave up. Others say they can't talk now, but will call me back, so I leave them a number. Sometimes, when I call again, they hang up and refuse to take my calls."

"What if that happens? What if she won't talk to

me? I need her, you know." Sarah fought down anxiety.

Mike studied her kindly. "All I can do is locate her for you, Sarah. I can't force her to meet with you."

"What if you locate her, but don't call her?" Sarah asked. "What if you just tell me where she is and I call her." She was thinking that it might be harder for Janelle to hang up on her own daughter.

"You're the client, and I'll handle it however you want me to."

Somehow, that made Sarah feel better, as if she had more control over the situation. "That's what I want you to do," she said. "Once you find her"—she didn't even think *if* you find her—"please call me. I want to be the first one to contact her."

Her mom grew rigid. "Sarah, that may not be possible. You may be back in the hospital, or—"

"I want to meet my mother face-to-face," Sarah interrupted.

Mike leaned back and jotted in a small black notebook. "No telling where she might live," he said. "It could be expensive for you to go confront her yourself."

"I have money," Sarah said stubbornly, again grateful to the faceless JWC for the gift.

"I don't think you should make those kinds of plans," Sarah's mother advised.

"I *have* to," Sarah countered, feeling her temper rising. "She's my mother. I need her."

Her father reached over and took his wife's hands. "Carol, honey, you know we agreed to help Sarah all we could. First, Mike has to locate the woman. Then, we can decide how best to handle it. Let's cross that bridge when we get to it."

Sarah's mom pressed her lips together and nodded without glancing at Sarah.

Mike flipped his notebook shut and clipped his silver ballpoint pen to his shirt pocket. "Don't be discouraged. Many times, these jobs of reconnecting birth families with adoptees turn out pretty good. Mine did."

"You were adopted?" Sarah asked. Except for Scott's friend, whom she only had heard about, she had never met anybody who actually had been adopted.

"I was," Mike said. "The people who adopted me were great parents, who told me all along I'd been adopted. I loved the Lions very much—I've even kept their name—but all my life, I wanted to meet the person who had given birth to me. I wanted brothers and sisters, blood relatives. Even after I married and had kids, I couldn't stop wanting to know who I was."

"So you searched?" Sarah asked.

He nodded. "That's how I got into this business. It used to be much more difficult to get information. Records of adoptions were closed and sealed. It took court orders and years of waiting to find out anything. As more and more people started searching, they became organized, formed support groups and organizations. These groups started applying political pressure and eventually loosened up the system. It's still not easy in some states, but people are recognizing adoptees' rights to have basic information about their genetic heritage."

He pushed his glasses up on his nose and studied Sarah thoughtfully. "For me, the search was a bonanza. I had six brothers and sisters on my natural mother's side and four on my father's. All of them were ecstatic to meet me, my wife, and my kids. We get together every two years for a huge family reunion.

"Now, I spend my life helping others find their birth families, because I know what it feels like to want to be connected by blood. The search can be frustrating. But every time you obtain information—a name, an address—it's like a small victory. And every time you hit a brick wall, it's like a small death."

Sarah felt as if a light had gone on inside her heart. Mike *did* understand—as only one who'd been adopted could understand. She was certain that her birth mother, Janelle Warren, had wondered about the daughter she'd given away fifteen years before. Once Sarah contacted her, Janelle might be shocked, but she would want to meet Sarah. And once she was tested for bone marrow compatibility, Janelle would be a match and would feel compelled to help Sarah.

No one could convince Sarah otherwise. Mothers and their children belonged to each other, no matter what had happened to separate them. The bond, the link could never be completely severed, regardless of time and circumstances. "I'll be at home waiting for your phone call," Sarah told the detective. "I know you'll find my mother. You must."

Thirteen

SARAH FOUND THAT the chemo treatments had taken their toll on her. She felt so weak and exhausted that she spent a great deal of time curled up on the sofa. It was hard to wait for Mike to contact them with more news. She wanted to conserve her energy for when she needed it to meet with her birth mother, so she didn't mind doing nothing much at all.

The waiting seemed longer since most of her friends had gone off on vacation. She was glad to get postcards, but felt sad to be reminded that while everyone was off having a good time, she was house-bound and bedridden.

"Mail call," Tina said, breezing toward her one morning.

"Anything important?" Sarah asked. For a moment, her heart hammered in anticipation, as it did every day when the mail arrived. Maybe this would be the day Mike would contact them.

"There's a package from New Mexico." Tina stared at a small box. "The address doesn't look familiar. Who do we know from there?"

Eagerly, Sarah took the box. It couldn't be from Mike. "It's from Scott," she said, feeling her disappointment dissolve immediately. "Remember, he went with his family to look at colleges and visit relatives in Santa Fe."

"Lucky him," Tina said.

Sarah felt a momentary stab of guilt. If it hadn't been for her search effort, the One Last Wish money could have been used for her family to go on a fabulous, luxurious vacation. Perhaps she was being selfish in not offering her parents some of the money to have a good time. "It's your money," her mom had told her. "Use it the way you must." Sarah hadn't offered any money because she honestly didn't know how long it would take to find her birth mother, or how expensive the search might be. Maybe when the search was over, maybe after her transplant, she could offer to take everyone on a trip.

"Aren't you going to open it?" Tina asked.

With a start, Sarah realized she'd been lost in thought. "Sure, I'm going to open it. Want to watch?" She could tell that Tina was interested.

Tina sat on the edge of the sofa and asked, "What do you think it is?"

Sarah shook the box. "Maybe it's some Indian beads. That's very popular stuff in Santa Fe."

"Open it already!"

Sarah pulled off the wrapping. Inside the small box was a bracelet of hammered silver, set with turquoise stones. "It's lovely," she said, thrilled that

Scott had not only thought of her, but sent her something so beautiful.

"I'll say," Tina declared, checking the bracelet over carefully. "Wish some guy as cute as Scott would send me a present."

"Someday, some guy will be falling all over you," Sarah told her, trying to be kind.

"Sure, if I stick my foot out and trip him."

Sarah laughed. She read Scott's note: "To the wonderful girl with eyes as blue as these stones. Scott." Sarah felt so happy, she blushed. Then, looking thoughtfully at her sister, she said, "Tina, you're pretty."

"Do you think so? I think my nose is too big."

"It looks like Mom's nose."

Tina rolled her eyes. "Oh, great. Why couldn't I have gotten one that looked more like yours?"

The comment was innocent enough, but their gazes tangled. Of course, there could never be a way for them to look alike—they weren't related. Tina dropped her gaze and shrugged. "You know what I mean."

"Sure," Sarah agreed hastily, not wanting the sisterly camaraderie to evaporate between them. It had been a while since they'd felt at ease around one another. "I know what you mean."

Tina stood. "I've got to split. I promised Mrs. Marcus I'd baby-sit Danny this morning."

Sarah felt a momentary twinge of jealousy. Babysitting Danny had always been her job. Now, she was too sick.

"Thanks for putting in a good word for me," Tina added. "If it hadn't been for you, she wouldn't have hired me. I'm saving my money for new school clothes."

"No problem," Sarah replied, with more cheerfulness than she felt. "Have fun." She watched Tina leave and settled back on the sofa with a sigh. She felt that life was passing her by, that everyone and everything was moving ahead.

She had little in common with her friends anymore. Cammie, Natalie, and JoEllen were a tight threesome, doing things together when they were home, and making plans for another year. Even Tina was thinking about the future. Sarah hardly let herself dwell on thoughts of tomorrow. Now, with the realization that she was adopted, she wondered if she'd ever had an honest past.

She thought about the enormous sum of money the anonymous JWC had given her. If only it could help her discover her past, then maybe she would have a future. She closed her eyes and prayed she'd hear from Mike soon.

Fourteen

Sarah slowly began to regain her strength. She hoped they would get more information from Mike while she was feeling better, because she'd have to return to the hospital soon for additional chemo, and she knew she'd be sick afterward. She was finding it more difficult to rally between treatments, and she wanted to be well and strong when she met her mother for the first time.

Dr. Hernandez called, concerned about Sarah's latest lab work. In spite of the treatments, cancer cells had reappeared in her bone marrow. "We're continuing to scan the registry in Sarah's behalf," Dr. Hernandez told Sarah's parents. "I'm afraid, however, we're not having any luck."

Sarah tried not to think that time was running out on her. Once they found her mother, things would be different. Her chances would be better. All she had to do was hold on until then. Sarah was half asleep when the phone rang late one night. Her father came into her room, bringing the cordless receiver to her. "It's Mike Lions," he said.

Instantly awake, Sarah took the phone while her father went downstairs and picked up the extension in the family room. "Hi," Sarah said, her voice breathless.

"I hope it's not too late for me to call."

"It's all right."

"I found Janelle Warren."

For a moment, Sarah couldn't speak. Her voice jammed in her throat, and her hands began to tremble. "Where are you, Mike?" she heard her father ask.

"Los Angeles. I found her living in one of the little beach communities near LA. She has a home and a well-established reputation in the town. It looks as if she'll be running for mayor in the fall elections."

Sarah felt a wave of delight spreading through her. Her mother might be famous. "You haven't said anything to her, have you?" Sarah asked suddenly.

"I've merely been observing her, checking on her discreetly," Mike assured Sarah. "I've spent hours in the local library's newspaper archives. What I've learned is, she's been a resident here since the early eighties—very successful in real estate and influential in local politics."

"Does she have a family?" Sarah's father asked.

"She's never married, although she's dating a rather prominent attorney at this time."

Sarah felt a sinking sensation in the pit of her stomach. She had no blood brothers or sisters, which meant that bone marrow compatibility had to depend entirely on her mother. Unless, of course, her mother could help her find her natural father.

"What do you want me to do?" Mike's question brought Sarah back to the present.

Her dad said, "My wife and Sarah and I will talk it over and get back to you tomorrow. Tell me how to reach you out there."

Sarah half heard the remainder of the conversation as her mind raced ahead with possibilities. When both her parents came into her room, she was waiting for them, sitting up in bed with her chin resting on her drawn-up knees. Her mom sat on the bed; her dad crossed his arms and leaned against the wall. Without giving them an opportunity to speak, Sarah blurted out, "I want to go to Los Angeles."

"Sarah, I don't think you should—" her mother began.

Sarah interrupted her. "I want to go."

"Your mother's right, honey. Maybe we should let Mike handle it. He's a professional, and he's best prepared to deal with this kind of situation."

"No. I want to meet her . . . talk to her face-to-face," Sarah insisted. She wanted to know why she'd been given away, but thought it best not to mention it.

Her mom glanced nervously toward her dad. "I would have to go with you. It would be a big expense."

Sarah waved her objection aside. "I have the money, remember? And it's all right if you come with me." Sarah realized she could never make the trip on her own. She would need help, especially if she got sick while she was out there. Her mom had dealt with her cancer for years and could handle anything that might occur. "But you can't get in the way of my meeting my mother," Sarah warned. "I know you don't want me to do this, but promise me you won't interfere."

Her mom looked stricken. "Sarah, this may be hard on my feelings, but I'm well aware it's your *life* we're trying to save. Of course, I won't get in the way."

Sarah felt agitated and restless. "How soon can we leave?" she asked.

"I-I don't know. . . . There's so much I'll have to do to prepare," her mother said. "I'll have to get someone to come in and watch Tina and Richie."

"Tina can handle it," Sarah replied.

"I don't think—"

"Stop treating her like a baby, Mom. You let her baby-sit for other people. She can look out for herself and Richie. She can cope in an emergency. You should let her do it. You can pay her with some of my One Last Wish money."

Her mother looked undecided as she nibbled on her bottom lip. "What do you think, Patrick?"

"Sarah's right. Tina's pretty capable." He thought a moment before continuing. "I'm right in the middle of some merger plans down at the office, but maybe I can put things on hold for a few days and come with you," he mused out loud.

"No," her mom protested. "I might be willing to let Tina manage during the daytime, but not nights. I don't want both of us out in California and the kids here alone."

He nodded in agreement. "Maybe you're right.

Mike will be out there with you, and if you need me, I can come."

Sarah listened while they made plans, barely able to contain her excitement. She was going to meet the woman who'd given birth to her, her *real* mother. Janelle might be surprised at Sarah's entrance into her life—maybe shocked by it—but after they met, after they talked, Sarah felt sure Janelle would be glad Sarah had contacted her. Perhaps she'd even want Sarah to become a permanent part of her life.

Tina's eyes were wide as saucers as, early the next morning, her mother explained what was about to happen. Sarah sat at the kitchen table, listening and toying with a spoon in a bowl of soggy cereal.

"You're going all the way out to California?" Tina asked her mother.

"It seems the only thing for us to do. Sarah needs to contact her—" she interrupted herself, "Ms. Warren as soon as possible. It may save time if Sarah goes to her personally."

Tina looked over at Sarah. "Gosh, I don't know what to say."

"Say you'll be all right here with Dad and Richie while we're gone," Sarah replied.

"I can take care of the three of us. I can cook—some. I can keep Richie entertained."

"I'll make up some casseroles and put them in the freezer," Mom said. "You can microwave them for suppers."

"How long will you be gone?"

"We're not sure."

Sarah kept her eyes on her cereal bowl. All the details were frustrating her. She simply wanted to get on a plane and leave. Tina asked, "What will you tell Richie?"

"I'll tell him we have to go away because of Sarah's illness. That's the basic truth."

"I'll talk to him," Sarah added. "I'll promise to bring him back a special surprise."

As their mom opened pantry doors and started making a grocery list, Tina turned to Sarah. "Are you nervous about meeting her?"

"Some." Actually, Sarah was extremely nervous.

"I hope she's nice to you."

"She'll be nice," Sarah said with more confidence than she felt.

"I wish there were something I could do to help."

"You're helping by taking care of Richie."

"I wish I could go with you."

"It's not exactly a vacation, Tina."

"I know, but I'd still like to go along. It seems exciting . . . going to Los Angeles."

Sarah stood, walked her bowl to the sink, and washed it out. Through the kitchen window, she saw the sloping backyard, bathed in sunlight that made the dew sparkle on the grass.

Later that day, Sarah told Richie about the trip. Immediately, he began to cry. "No! No, Sarah! Don't go."

"It's just for a little while," she assured him. She hugged him tightly and promised him toys and T-shirts. "Now, don't cry. We'll be back soon."

He clung to her and let go only when she took him to her room to sit on her bed while she packed. He watched her as she moved around the room, selecting outfits, discarding others. What did a person wear to meet one's mother for the first time, she wondered.

Richie lay his favorite stuffed bear on top of her things. "He wants to go, too," Richie said.

"I shouldn't take him. He might miss you."

Richie shook his head. "He wants to go."

A lump rose in Sarah's throat as she gazed down at the scuffed-up, well-loved bear. "Sing me a song," she asked Richie, forcing cheeriness. "One of your favorites."

His voice trembled as he sang, "There was a farmer had a dog, and Bingo was his name-o . . ."

Sarah continued to pack for the reunion of her life.

Fifteen

⌒⌒

THE PLANE KNIFED through a bank of white clouds as Sarah stared out the window. Below, the city of Los Angeles sprawled in a haphazard maze of neighborhoods and buildings, broken by dark lines of roads and freeways as far as she could see.

"Are you feeling better?" her mother asked from the seat beside Sarah.

"A little," Sarah said. She had felt nauseated most of the trip, partly because of anxiety. Her wig was making her scalp itch, and there was now a small drop of blood staining the front of her blouse where the Broviac catheter, still implanted in her chest, had caught on her bra. "I'll be glad when we're on the ground."

"Me, too. Four hours on an airplane is quite enough for me."

Mike Lions was waiting at the gate as Sarah and her mother deplaned. He shook their hands and eased Sarah's duffel bag off her shoulder. "Let me take this."

"We have more."

Mike grinned. "I'm not surprised. My wife can't travel across the street without two pieces of luggage."

It took another two hours for them to gather their luggage, get to Mike's rental car, and drive to the hotel where he'd reserved Sarah and her mom a room. Once there, he ordered a platter of fresh fruit and cold drinks from room service. Sarah stretched out on the bed and sipped her cola, grateful for the relief the air-conditioning provided from the relentless California summer heat.

"Let me tell you what I've got," Mike said without preamble. "Janelle Warren is the head of a small real estate agency that's been very successful. As I told you on the phone, she's planning to run for mayor, and from what I hear, it's going to be a really tough fight. The man she's trying to unseat has been mayor for twelve years."

"You said she has no family," Mrs. McGreggor said. She and Mike sat at a small round table across from Sarah's bed.

"She lives quietly, in a modest house, with two cats and a parrot," Mike replied.

Suddenly, Sarah spoke up. "I want to see her."

"You will," her mom promised. "You should get some rest before we go out in this heat again."

"That's not what I mean. I want to *see* her before I meet her. Before I introduce myself to her, I just want to look at her." Sarah couldn't explain why it was important to her, but it was. Somehow, she had to reconcile her fantasies with the flesh-and-blood person before she actually met her.

Mike tapped the tabletop while he considered Sarah's request. "I've been shadowing her, so I'm pretty familiar with her habits. We could have lunch tomorrow at the place where she usually eats. That way, you could get a good look at her without her knowing."

"You mean spy on her?" her mom asked sharply.

"Observe," Mike corrected.

"That's what I'd like to do," Sarah said. "I'd like to observe her." She preferred Mike's choice of words.

"If that's what you want, then that's what we'll do." Mike stood up. "Why don't the two of you get some rest, and I'll phone you in the morning. If we leave here by nine, we can drive down the coast and be at the restaurant before she arrives."

Without waiting for her mom's approval of the plan, Sarah agreed. She fell asleep before the door clicked shut behind Mike.

The next morning, Mike drove them along a road that hugged the shoreline of the Pacific Ocean. Individual communities blended into one another, but finally, he pulled into a parking lot in a small downtown area. "Feel up to walking some?" he asked. "You might like to look around the city a bit. The restaurant we're going to is a few blocks over."

By the time the three of them had entered the restaurant for lunch, Sarah was so nervous that her stomach felt tied in knots. Her mom ordered her some crackers, which Sarah nibbled on halfheartedly. Mike scanned the menu and made suggestions, but Sarah was in no mood to eat. As it got closer to noon, the restaurant began to fill up. Sarah asked, "What if she decides not to come here today?"

"Then we'll go by her office," Mike said. "Relax. She'll be here." He was looking toward the doorway when Sarah saw his eyes narrow.

Quickly, she looked up. In the doorway stood a tall, slim woman with stylish, short blond hair. Mike didn't have to tell Sarah she was seeing Janelle Warren. She would have known her mother anywhere. Sarah's heart thudded, and her mouth went perfectly dry. "There she is," Sarah whispered.

Mike nodded confirmation.

Sarah watched as a waiter led Janelle to a table, where a distinguished-looking man with steel gray hair stood and pulled out a chair for her. "The boyfriend," Mike explained. Sarah thought Mike's term an odd one to use for people who were adults. Teenagers were boyfriend and girlfriend—not grown-ups.

Sarah couldn't take her eyes off her mother. She seemed so elegant and poised. Back in Sarah's hometown, the women were so ordinary. Her mom's friends wore sweats and sneakers, jeans and casual shirts to the grocery store and to PTA meetings. Women like Janelle, who dressed in silk and linen suits were glamorous and exciting. For a moment, Sarah felt dazzled.

"You should eat something," Carol McGreggor said when the waiter brought their lunch.

Sarah ate automatically, hardly tasting the soup and salad placed in front of her. She couldn't take her eyes off her birth mother. Every move Janelle made, the way she held her fork, the way she tossed her head when she laughed, seemed magical to Sarah. A part of her wanted to rush over and throw her arms around Janelle's neck. She wanted to shout, "I'm your daughter! Your only daughter."

Another part of her trembled in fear. What would her mother's reaction be? Would she be pleased to see her? Would she embrace her? Had she ever missed having Sarah in her life? "I'm not sure what to do," Sarah confessed to Mike. "What should I do?"

"It would be best to approach her when she's alone," Mike replied.

"When will she be alone?"

"Maybe when she goes home tonight. Are you sure you don't want to contact her by phone first? It might be less awkward."

Sarah shook her head emphatically. After having seen Janelle, she couldn't resort to the impersonal use of the telephone. "Can we follow her when she leaves?" Sarah asked, feeling a peculiar need to be near her birth mother.

"That's not a good idea," Mrs. McGreggor said. "It seems sneaky to me. Besides, you should get some rest this afternoon."

"I don't want to rest. I want to be with my mother," she insisted.

Her mom looked as if she'd been slapped. "It was only a suggestion."

Before anything else could be said, Sarah saw Janelle and her lunch companion rise. "Look. They're leaving." Sarah felt an edge of panic. "I don't want to lose her."

"It's all right," Mike assured her. "We'll keep pace behind her."

Sarah could tell her mom didn't want to do such a thing. Still, Mrs. McGreggor rose and tagged along

when Sarah and Mike stepped out onto the sidewalk.

"Don't crowd her," Mike cautioned.

Sarah kept her eyes on Janelle as she ambled
along the sidewalk. Janelle walked with confidence,
greeting people along the way. The walk to her office
was short, and when Janelle stepped inside, Sarah
felt disoriented. She didn't want to lose sight of her.

"Her habits are regular as clockwork," Mike said.
"She'll head home about six o'clock, and we can be
there waiting for her."

"Perhaps we can take in a movie," Mrs. McGreggor offered. "It will pass the time and get Sarah out
of the heat of the day."

Reluctantly, Sarah agreed. The three of them sat
through a film, and as soon as it was over, Sarah
headed for Mike's car. He drove her and her mom
into a quiet neighborhood where palm trees lined
the streets and exotic tropical flowers bloomed on
bushes and trellises. Sarah scarcely saw the lush sce-
nery, she was so preoccupied.

Mike parked across the street from a white stucco
house with a red Spanish tile roof and a red tile
porch. "That's it," he told them.

Minutes later, Sarah watched as a car swung into
the driveway and Janelle emerged from the driver's
side. "I guess this is it," Sarah remarked, after giving
Janelle a little time to get inside. Now that the time
had come to meet her mother, Sarah grew appre-
hensive. She struggled to find courage to approach
the house.

"I could go with you," her mom ventured.

"I want to go alone."

"If you need me . . ."

"I won't." Sarah stepped away from the car and walked slowly across the street, up the walk, and onto the porch. The scent of gardenias and summer roses mingled in the humid air. Her finger trembled as she poked the doorbell. From within, she heard a chime. Moments later, the door opened and she was looking into the face of Janelle Warren—the face of her biological mother.

Sixteen

◦~◦

SARAH'S KNEES SHOOK, and her tongue felt stuck to the roof of her mouth. Janelle gazed at her expectantly. "Is it Girl Scout cookie time already?" she asked with a smile.

Sarah experienced a sinking sensation in the pit of her stomach. Janelle didn't even recognize her own flesh and blood! "No," Sarah managed to say.

"Are you lost?" Janelle frowned.

"I'm S-Sarah," Sarah stammered.

"Yes?"

Sarah silently scolded herself. Of course, the name *Sarah* wouldn't mean anything. Desperately, she searched for a way to express who she was. "You knew me as 'Baby Girl Warren' when I was born."

The color drained from Janelle Warren's face. Her eyes darted nervously over Sarah's head and she blurted out, "Go away!"

"But I want—"

"Get out of here. I don't know you. I don't know what you're talking about. Go away!" Janelle slammed the door in Sarah's face.

Stunned, Sarah stood on the porch, unable to move. She felt as if someone had hurled a brick at her. Her knees buckled, and she grabbed for the door for support. Suddenly, Mike and her mom were beside her, leading her away from the porch.

"What happened?" her mom demanded.

"She told me to go away. She said she didn't know me and didn't want to, either. Sarah felt like a robot—her emotions were frozen.

"I was afraid of this. The shock was too much," Mike said. "Maybe if I explain things to Janelle Warren . . ."

"No! We're going back to the hotel," Carol McGreggor said forcefully. "Now, we do it my way, not Sarah's."

Sarah didn't argue. She felt foolish. The sound of a slamming door reverberated in her ears, the hostile, fearful look on Janelle's face indelibly stamped in her memory. *Go away!* she'd been ordered. *Go away!* Sarah got into the backseat of Mike's car, and her mom climbed in next to her. Even though the evening air was warm, her teeth began to chatter and she felt chilly.

Back in their hotel room, Sarah crossed to the window and opened the heavy drape. She heard Mike and her mom talking quietly. Then the door closed, and Mike was gone. "You tried to warn me, but I wouldn't listen," Sarah said bitterly. "Go ahead and say, 'I told you so.' "

"I'm sorry, Sarah."

A tear trickled down Sarah's cheek, and she

reached up and wiped it away. "She said she didn't know me."

"Sarah, I'm not defending her, but your showing up on her doorstep after fifteen years must have been quite a shock for her."

"She hates me. My real mother hates me."

Her mom touched her shoulder and turned her around, her face dark with anger. "Stop talking like that, Sarah, and listen to me. Your *real* mother loves you. I know that's true, because I'm your *real* mother. I'm tired of your pretending otherwise. Why wasn't I enough for you, Sarah? What's wrong with me?"

Sarah blinked, caught off guard by the heat in her mom's voice. "Nothing's wrong with you."

"Then stop treating me like a second-class person. As if I'm somehow inferior because you didn't drop out of my body." Her voice rose with intensity. "*I'm* your real mother. I was the one who held your hand when you took your first steps. I was the one who took you to your first day of school and held you when you cried. I was the one who was with you when the doctors diagnosed leukemia. I sat through the tests with you. I wept with you, prayed with you, stayed nights in the hospital with you. It was *me*, Sarah. Not Janelle Warren. It was *me*—I am your mother."

As she listened, a jumble of childhood memories tumbled through Sarah's mind, as if she were watching a speeded-up video. She saw herself in the hospital with lab technicians jabbing her with long syringes while her mother held her hand and stroked her cheek.

"I didn't mean to be ungrateful." Sarah hoped desperately that her mother knew she meant it.

"Ungrateful!" Mrs. McGreggor fairly shouted. "Is that what you think I want from you? Your gratitude? Grow up, Sarah. We are *family*. All of us—your dad, Tina, Richie, me. You belong to us, not by virtue of some piece of legal paper, but because we chose you, raised you, loved you."

Suddenly, Sarah felt herself growing angry. "You never wanted me to look for Janelle. You would never have even told me that I was adopted if it wasn't for the bone marrow transplant."

"You bet I didn't want you to look for her. I was afraid of her, Sarah. Afraid that she was better than I am, more interesting and exciting. Look at me. I'm short and fat and boring. I've been a housewife and a mother all my life. My family *is* my life and is all I ever wanted. Until today. I saw Janelle in that restaurant, too, you know. I saw how your eyes lit up. And it made me feel so . . . inadequate."

Her mom's confession surprised Sarah. She hadn't expected jealousy and envy. "I don't think you're inferior to her. That's not it at all. It's just . . . I've told you before . . . I'm curious about her," Sarah insisted.

"Curious is one thing, but this fascination you've carried around has been unfair. It's hateful and punishing." Her mom turned and walked to the far side of the hotel room. "All these months, I've felt so threatened by her."

"How could you? You didn't even know her."

"I had this idea that she'd steal you away. What right did she have to you?"

"Steal me? She won't even talk to me."

"She's stolen you, all right," her mom countered. "You've spent the last three months consumed with locating her—and not just because of the bone marrow, either."

"I need to know who I am."

"I'll tell you who you are. You're Sarah Louise McGreggor, and have been since you were three days old."

"No . . . Maybe my name is Sarah McGreggor, but *I* am part of Janelle Warren and my natural father. There's a difference. I'm different from Tina and Richie, from you and Dad. Why can't you understand what I've been going through?"

"Why can't you understand what *I've* been going through?"

As they stood glaring at each other, Sarah realized how deeply her preoccupation with her birth mother had wounded her mom. While she had fantasized about her birth mother, her mom had felt rejected. Sarah recalled Tina's trying to tell her as much. "I'm sorry if I've hurt you. It's just that the One Last Wish money seemed to give me a way to have everything—my birth mother, the bone marrow, you, Dad, Tina and Richie . . ." Sarah's voice trailed, thick with unshed tears.

Her mother gripped the back of a chair. "That Wish money could have given our family wonderful things. But now, as far as I'm concerned, it was a curse."

"How can you say that? It's a ton of money, and it's paid for all of this."

"Contrary to popular belief, Sarah, money doesn't buy everything. In this case, for me, it's bought a boatload of unhappiness."

Sarah remembered what she'd explained to Scott—that she wanted to know the truth, she wanted to trade lies and fantasy for reality. He had tried to caution her that sometimes the truth hurt and might be better left undisturbed. Now, she understood what he was trying to tell her, but it was too late.

Her mom shrugged. "At the time, we thought we were doing the right thing by respecting your birth mother's wishes and keeping your adoption a secret. If I had known it would cause so much pain on both our sides, I would have never agreed to secrecy." She crossed the room and flipped the wall switch on. "Regardless of how things were handled, we're here now," her mom said. "Sadly, despite the way Janelle treated you today, you still need her. Get your purse. I'm calling Mike, and you and I are going back to see her."

"She won't talk to us."

"Yes, she will," her mom said. Her eyes looked steely hard, and her voice sounded determined. "Whether Janelle Warren likes it or not, fifteen years ago she gave birth to a baby. Now, that child needs her. She won't walk away from you this time, Sarah—I won't let her. You need her bone marrow, and I'm going to tell her so."

Seventeen

SARAH WASN'T NEARLY as afraid the second time she stood on Janelle Warren's porch as she'd been the first time. This time, her mom and Mike were standing shoulder-to-shoulder with her. The worst had already happened—she'd been rejected by her birth mother.

When the door opened, Janelle stared at them incredulously. Light from her living room flooded through the doorway. "I told you I don't want to be bothered," Janelle said. "Please go away."

"We can't do that," Sarah heard her mom reply. "We must talk to you."

"If you don't go away, I'll call the police," Janelle insisted.

Sarah watched Janelle's knuckles turn white as she gripped the door frame. "Ms. Warren," Mike began to explain, "We're not here to harm you or make trouble for you. I'm a private investigator, and these people want to talk to you . . . *need* to talk to you."

"Your standing here is harming me," Janelle replied.

"Ms. Warren," Sarah's mom said, "believe me, this is very difficult on all of us. I can assure you, we'll be going just as soon as we talk to you. Sarah doesn't really have a choice about this. Without your help, she may die."

Janelle didn't say anything. She gazed at Sarah, who felt insignificant by the inspection. "All right." Janelle spoke in a suspicious voice. "Come in, but make it brief. I'm expecting company." She opened the door wider.

"I'll wait out in the car," Mike told Sarah and her mom. "You don't need me anymore."

Sarah stayed close to her mom as Janelle led them inside the house. Sarah looked around. She noticed wall-to-wall white carpeting. Janelle led them into a beautifully decorated room, filled with expensive objects arranged on polished wood tables and sparkling glass shelves. She motioned for them to sit, and Sarah noted the lush, elegant cream-color sofa. Janelle took a chair opposite them. "What do you want?" she asked stiffly.

I want you to look at me, Sarah felt like saying. *I want you to tell me who I am and where I came from.* "This is as awkward for me as it is for you," Carol McGreggor began. "I never dreamed I'd ever have to meet you, face you."

"I believe not meeting me was a condition of the adoption," Janelle said coolly.

"My parents never told me I was adopted," Sarah said, somehow feeling defensive toward her mom and dad. "I just found out when I was told about my medical problem."

"Then you understood that I didn't want to be found? Yet, you came looking for me, anyway."

"We told her your wishes, too," Carol assured Janelle. "We understood them from the day we signed the papers, and we respected them until we had no choice."

Janelle sat forward on the edge of the chair. "You had no right to come here." She turned toward Sarah. "I had my reasons for giving you up. Very good reasons. It wasn't easy, you know. But what's done is done. There's no turning back."

Sarah didn't believe what she was hearing. Janelle made it sound as if it had been easy and final. "What were your reasons? I deserve to know."

Janelle looked startled. Abruptly, she stood. "I don't have to defend my choices to anyone. Giving you up was *my* choice. Believe me, the Supreme Court had already legalized abortion, and I was certainly free to take that route. An abortion doesn't show on a woman's body the way a pregnancy does, you know."

Sarah wondered if she was supposed to feel grateful because Janelle had elected to have her instead of getting an abortion. "I'm sorry I was such an inconvenience," Sarah snapped. She couldn't hide her anger. Maybe it was better for her to feel angry, so it hurt less.

"I have a very good life now," Janelle told them.

"And you don't need me complicating it," Sarah finished.

"I don't mean to sound cruel or heartless. I'm sure you've been curious about your background. I just don't think I can help you. I have a high profile in this community. The man I'm seeing seriously is being considered for a judgeship. Even a hint of scandal could be ruinous to both of us, even in this day and age. Certainly, for him it would change things. I can't do that to myself. I don't want to."

Sarah felt as if she'd been spat on. Janelle was worried about her reputation? If she didn't feel so heartbroken, she might have laughed.

"We didn't come here to ruin your reputation," Carol insisted. "I told you we're here for Sarah's sake, and that's the truth. Perhaps she looks healthy to you, but Sarah has leukemia."

Janelle sat forward, her eyes wide, but she didn't soften. She held her body rigid. "I am sorry."

Carol waved her comment aside. "I'll get to the point. Sarah has been in remission, but now she's had a relapse. Her doctors have told us that her best hope is a bone marrow transplant, and the best donor would be a blood relative—preferably a brother or sister."

"There are none." Janelle's voice was barely a whisper.

"That's what Mike Lions, our detective, has told us. Therefore, the only candidate left is you."

"Or my natural father," Sarah added hopefully. "Maybe he has children."

Janelle's face looked bloodless, and for a moment, Sarah thought she might crumble. "He doesn't," she said tersely.

Sarah waited for some other word about the man who had fathered her, but none was forthcoming. Carol said, "Then that leaves you. The test to check for compatibility is a simple one. A lab draws blood—"

"I can't help you," Janelle interrupted.

"What?"

Janelle turned and walked to a large picture window and toyed with the drapery cord. The curtains were already shut, *just like Janelle Warren's heart*, Sarah thought.

"I'm very sorry for you, but there's nothing I can do," Janelle said. "It's quite impossible. Really."

"I see," Sarah's mom said, and stood up.

Sarah didn't "see" at all. All she knew was that the woman who'd opted to bear her fifteen years before was now refusing to have a blood test for bone marrow compatibility. Sarah felt sick to her stomach. How could Janelle hate Sarah so much that she didn't want to know her or help her? Perhaps it would have been more merciful if she had had an abortion. Sarah's sense of rejection was unbearable.

An awkward silence hung in the air, broken only by the ticking of a grandfather clock. "Well, we've taken enough of your time," Carol said finally. "I know you're expecting company."

Janelle nervously glanced at the clock. "Yes. He should be here soon."

"And we wouldn't want to have to explain who we are, would we?" Carol's tone was cutting.

Two bright spots of color appeared on Janelle's cheeks, but she said nothing. Sarah rose beside her mom and watched as she opened her purse. She put a piece of paper atop the coffee table. "This is the hotel where we're staying. I've also written down the name and phone number of Sarah's doctor in Memphis. If you want to discuss anything with her, feel free to call."

She snapped her purse closed and started to the door. Janelle didn't move, and neither did Sarah. They gazed at each other across the beautifully furnished living room. Janelle's eyes looked pained, but she made no move to stop Sarah and Carol from leaving. Sarah's knees felt rubbery and weak, yet she crossed to the door, her head held high. From there, she followed her mom out into the night.

Sarah's tears didn't start until they got back to the hotel room. She climbed into the shower stall, turned on the water, and let them flow. *Janelle honestly didn't want her.* She had cut Sarah out of her life and offered no hope for a future. When she came out of the bathroom, her mom rose from a chair and opened her arms. Without a second's hesitation, Sarah rushed to them. Her mom held her, rocked her, and told her, "It'll be all right, honey. I love you. Dad loves you. We've told you, we are your true family."

Sarah needed the words, soaking them up like a sponge. Through her sobs, she said, "What now, Mom? Without Janelle, I'll die. Mom, please help me. I don't want to die."

Eighteen

∽❦∽

THE NEXT MORNING, there was nothing left to do but pack to go home. Sarah felt weighted down, her legs so heavy that she could barely lift them to move around the room. Her mother kept trying to be cheerful, supportive, just as she'd been the night before. Her mom had insisted, "You're not going to die, honey. You're just disappointed about your birth mother. After a good night's sleep, you'll feel better. Things will look better in the morning."

Sarah was so distraught, she didn't know what to feel. Nothing could ever take away the sense of abandonment and rejection she felt. As her mom packed, she told Sarah, "Your father will meet our plane in Atlanta and drive us home. Tina and Richie are excited about seeing you. They've all missed you terribly, Sarah. I think Tina's planning a party for you with some of your friends."

"I really don't want a party. I don't want to explain things to people."

"As far as everyone knows, Sarah, we took a trip to California for medical reasons. No one knows about your adoption."

Now that things had turned out the way they had, Sarah was glad she'd decided to keep her adoption a secret. At the time, she'd thought she'd done it for Tina. As it turned out, she'd done it for herself.

There was a knock on the door. Her mother glanced at her watch. "Mike's early. Sarah, tell him we're not ready and to come back in about an hour."

Sarah opened the door, but it wasn't Mike standing in the hall. It was Janelle Warren. "Can I come in?" Janelle asked.

"What do you want?" Sarah's mom swooped alongside of Sarah protectively.

"To talk."

Reluctantly, Sarah backed away from the door so that Janelle could enter. "What do you want to talk about?" Sarah asked as Janelle walked to the large window and turned to face her.

"I was up most of the night thinking about our meeting. I feel that I owe you some kind of explanation," Janelle said.

"We're leaving pretty soon, so you don't have to worry about me spoiling your life. I'm sorry I bothered you," Sarah said sharply.

"I'm sorry I wasn't more cordial to you. It was such a shock seeing you, knowing who you were."

"Especially since you'd always thought I was out of your life forever." Sarah's tone was challenging.

Janelle carefully set her expensive-looking handbag on the table. "You may have been out of my life, Sarah, but you were never forgotten."

"It didn't seem that way yesterday."

"A woman doesn't give birth to a baby and erase the experience from her mind—or her heart. It's especially difficult every year on your birthday. I carried you for nine months. I was in labor with you for twelve hours. I held you for ten minutes before they took you away. I walked out of the hospital with empty arms, while other women took their newborns home. It was one of the hardest things I have ever had to do."

Sarah was skeptical. "But you did it."

"I thought it best that you have a good home, with *two* parents. I couldn't give you that." Janelle glanced toward Carol. "You did go to a good home, Sarah. I'm sure of it."

Carol moved closer to Sarah. "I love Sarah very much."

Janelle studied the two of them. "It shows."

"I have a good home," Sarah confirmed. "Is that all you want to say?"

Janelle opened her purse and pulled out some photographs. "Since I know you've come a long way, and I understand your desire to know something of your heritage, I've brought some things to show you." She laid the photos on the table.

Sarah edged closer and peered at the black-and-white photos. The first was of a run-down shack with old junk cars sitting on the barren ground of the yard. "This is where I grew up, in the heart of the Ozarks," Janelle explained. "Mom and Pop had eight children. Two died from scarlet fever when they were babies—something that can be easily cured with penicillin, but my folks had no money for medicine, and the nearest doctor lived in the next county."

Sarah was shocked at the condition of the house, unable to picture the elegant woman in front of her growing up in such poverty. Neither could she imagine not being able to afford medicine for a sick child. "You lived there?"

"Until I was sixteen. We didn't even have indoor plumbing. We got along by farming a garden, and sometimes my dad got work as a hired hand. My parents were good people, Sarah, but ignorant and uneducated. I loved school from the first day I walked into a classroom. It didn't take me long to figure out that if I didn't want to end up like my parents, I had to get a good education. Fortunately, I was bright and really did well in the classroom."

Janelle showed Sarah another picture. It was a blurred group shot of a man and a woman standing on the porch with a cluster of blond-headed kids around them. "My kinfolk," Janelle continued. Her fine, cultured speech had taken on a hint of her Ozark roots.

"I was the only Warren up to that time to graduate from high school. All the others quit school as soon as they were old enough, so they could work. It was a proud moment for me. An even prouder moment when I learned I'd been awarded a full four-year academic scholarship to the University of Arkansas.

"I remember how the whole family came down to the bus depot and sent me off. I cried all the way to Little Rock, but I never looked back. I was doing the only thing I could to make something out of my life."

"You were happy?" Sarah asked.

"I was happy. I did well in college. Earned top grades, special honors. I wanted to be an attorney, and after I graduated, I was accepted to law school on scholarship."

"But you didn't become a lawyer?"

"No. I wanted that scholarship in the worst way, but . . ." Janelle's voice trailed off.

"But instead, you had me," Sarah finished.

"I had you," Janelle confirmed. She stared at another photo for a moment, then placed it on the table. It was of a handsome, brown-haired man with a cocky smile. "This is your father. His name was Trevor Benedict. He was training to be a navy pilot when I met him on a spring break trip to Pensacola, Florida. I'd never been in love before, and I'll tell you now, I've never been in love like that since then."

Carol had leaned over to peer at the picture. "Sarah looks like him through the eyes," she commented. "And she has the same kind of cleft in her chin."

Sarah was too mesmerized to see the resemblance herself. Merely being able to look on the face of the man who had fathered her was making her heart hammer wildly. "Didn't he want to marry you when you told him about me?" she asked. It was a bold question, but she wanted to know all she could about him.

"I never told him," Janelle said. Sarah looked up quickly and saw that Janelle's eyes were shimmering with tears. "He was killed in a flight training accident before I could tell him. His fighter jet hit the ground and exploded."

Horrified, Sarah felt her own eyes well up with tears. She heard her mom gasp. Janelle pushed the photo aside. "I was devastated. If I hadn't been pregnant, I might have killed myself. At the time, my options were very few. I couldn't not have you—you were all that was left of him. I couldn't go back home—my folks had such pride in me. They didn't know I was pregnant, and I didn't want them to know. In those days, there was a certain amount of shame in being an unwed mother. Women didn't wear illegitimate pregnancies like badges of pride, as they do today. Adoption seemed like the best solution."

"Yet, your instructions about anonymity were so explicit," Sarah's mom said. "I believed that you didn't want anything to do with your baby."

"I knew it had to be a clean break. I assumed that if I sounded threatening about it, she would never come searching for me." Janelle's voice took on a softness. "I see I was wrong. It didn't deter you at all."

Sarah felt sad and a bit overwhelmed by what she'd heard. Perhaps her mom had been right: Using the One Last Wish money to search for her roots had upset the lives of many people—and it had all come to nothing.

"As you know, Sarah didn't initiate this search frivolously," Carol McGreggor said. "Her father and I wouldn't have helped her if she hadn't had a very pressing reason for finding you."

Janelle nodded with understanding. "Yes . . . the

bone marrow. I called and spoke with your doctor, Sarah. She explained more fully about the transplant."

"Will you take the test for compatibility then?" Sarah felt a resurgence of hope.

"It won't matter if I am compatible, Sarah. Dr. Hernandez can't use my marrow. I'm not a suitable candidate."

"Why not?" The hope seemed to be slipping through her fingers like sand.

"Several years ago, I had a lump removed from my breast. It was cancerous. I underwent chemo and radiation, and even though I've been cancer-free for the past three years, I can never be a bone marrow donor. Not for you, not for anyone."

To Sarah, it seemed as if a giant iron door had closed and locked her in a cage. "Breast cancer?" she asked, thunderstruck.

Janelle gave Sarah a long, sad look. "My doctors told me the disease has a tendency to run in families—my mother, your grandmother, died from uterine cancer. I hoped the tendency would stop with me. I never dreamed it had been passed on to you. I'm so very, very sorry, Sarah."

Sarah could think of nothing to say. As she stood in the room with her mother and her mom, she felt as if she'd come to the end of a long journey, a journey that had brought her to the edge of a future she couldn't navigate.

"I'm sorry, too. For you and for Sarah," Carol said, stepping to Sarah's side. She put her arm protectively around Sarah's shoulders. "Thank you for taking the time to come by and tell us all of this. It was kind of you, and I know it means a great deal to Sarah."

Janelle picked up her purse and draped the strap over her shoulder. "As I told you, I felt you both deserved some kind of explanation. I didn't want you to leave thinking I hated you."

Sarah's throat felt swollen shut as she nodded her understanding.

Janelle walked to the door, where she turned and gazed longingly at Sarah. "Could you . . . would you mind terribly if I hugged you good-bye?" she asked.

Sarah glanced at her mom, who dropped her arm from Sarah's shoulders. Slowly, Sarah stepped forward to face the woman who had borne her, and who had given her up for adoption. Janelle's arms slipped around her, and Sarah felt herself pulled closer. The scent of Janelle's lovely perfume filled Sarah's senses as she closed her eyes and slowly wound her arms around her mother. They stood motionless in the quiet of the room while Sarah searched inside herself for something to link them. She could not find one memory of this woman to whom she was bound by blood.

Janelle released her, letting her hands slide along Sarah's arms until she was holding Sarah's hands. Tears glistened in her eyes as she studied Sarah's face. "I haven't held you since you were a tiny baby. Since the nurse brought you to me and laid you in my arms," Janelle whispered. "Now, you're all grown up."

She dropped Sarah's hands. "I'll leave you the photos, Sarah. They're your birthright, you know. When I put you up for adoption, I was certain I'd never see you again. In the long run, I'm glad I was able to meet you, and I truly regret not being able to help you. You're a lovely young woman, and I know your parents are very proud of you."

Sarah watched her open the door and, without a backward glance, slip silently into the hall and out of her life.

Nineteen

SARAH AND HER mom arrived home to a party arranged by Tina. Scott threw his arms around Sarah and talked excitedly. She listened to their chatter, but felt as if she weren't a part of their world anymore.

She was sitting on the steps of the front porch, moodily watching a sprinkler spew water on the front lawn, when Scott brought her a piece of Tina's homemade chocolate cake. She thanked him for the cake and for the bracelet he'd sent. "I thought about you a lot this summer, and about what you were going through," he said, lowering himself to the front stoop. "I guess things didn't work out between you and your birth mother."

"Not really. I'm glad I met her, even though, at first, she wasn't too thrilled about my arrival on her doorstep."

Tina stole quietly up beside Sarah and sat on the

porch step below Scott. There was a time when Sarah would have resented her intrusion, but now she didn't care. She wanted Tina to hear, uncertain that she was up to telling the story more than once. She was feeling hot and achy all over, and a headache pounded behind her eyes.

"What's she like?" Tina asked.

Sarah gave the highlights of her trip and of the conversations with her birth mother. "The big reunion wasn't easy on any of us," Sarah said.

"I can't believe she can't be a bone marrow donor for you."

"That was the hardest part of all. I have to admit, I was really counting on her helping me out in that department."

"What happens now?" Tina asked, looking worried.

"I don't know." Sarah felt defeated, as if time was running out on her. "I guess they have to keep trying that bone marrow registry."

"I wish I could help," Tina said.

"Me, too," Scott said.

The screen door flew open, and Richie bounded out onto the porch. He had chocolate frosting still smeared on his face. "Sarah," he said with a beaming smile, "come and see what I made for you."

Sarah held him at arm's length. "Slow down, buster. You didn't tell me how you liked having Tina for a mommy while Mom and I were gone."

Richie sneaked a peek at Tina. "She was bossy. She made me pick up my toys every night."

"That doesn't sound so terrible."

Richie shrugged. "She read me stories before bed and let me help her fix breakfast."

Sarah glanced at her sister, who grinned. Tina looked older to her, more mature, not so much the thirteen-year-old pain in the neck she'd been months before. Sarah wondered if it was Tina who'd changed, or she herself. She turned back to Richie. "What did you make for me?"

"A necklace out of clay." His small face broke into a giant grin.

"Show me." Sarah stood, but she felt woozy.

Richie grabbed her hand, then dropped it. "You're *hot*, Sarah."

Her mother was just coming out on the porch. Concern replaced the smile on her face. "Are you all right?" she asked, feeling Sarah's forehead.

Sarah swayed and grabbed the porch rail. She noticed how cool her mother's hand felt on her skin. "Why, you're burning up!" her mother exclaimed. "You get into bed right this minute. I'm calling the doctor."

Scott and Tina helped her up to her room. She heard Richie ask, "Is Sarah sick again?"

The noises of the afternoon faded in and out as Sarah shivered under the covers. No matter how many blankets they put on her, she couldn't get warm. By nightfall, her mother came into her room and began to pack a suitcase. "Dr. Hernandez wants us to bring you to Memphis right away."

"We haven't even unpacked from California yet," Sarah protested through chattering teeth.

"You're sick, honey, and she wants you in the hospital. Dad's fixing the backseat of the car with pillows so that you'll be more comfortable for the trip."

Sarah felt like crying. She didn't want to go back

to the lonely days and nights of the hospital. She wanted to stay home. She wanted to start school on the first day of classes. She wanted to be well. She thought about the money and JWC's letter and the part that said JWC's granted wish had brought purpose, faith, and courage. The fulfillment of Sarah's wish had brought only a bittersweet reunion, frustration, and fear. She still had no bone marrow to save her. No amount of money could buy that.

Scott poked his head through the doorway, concern written all over his face. "You going to be all right?"

"Sure," Sarah lied. "Can't keep me down."

He crouched next to her bed and ran the back of his hand across her cheek. "You'd better be all right. Who's going to be my personal trainer when school starts?"

"Maybe you'd better start looking for someone else."

"No way. You're my fiancée, remember?"

She smiled, but the effort hurt. "I release you to choose another."

"Maybe I don't want to be released."

She reached up and touched his hair. "Don't hold me to a promise I can't keep."

Scott's eyes clouded. He kissed her cheek and stood stiffly. "No deal," he said. "A promise is a promise."

How wonderful it would have been to grow up and marry Scott Michaels. How wonderful—and now, how impossible.

When Scott had gone, Tina came in to see her, looking scared.

"Thanks for the party," Sarah said.

Tina's eyes filled with tears. "It wasn't supposed to end this way. It was supposed to be a happy homecoming."

Home. For Sarah, the word had a whole new meaning. Home was here, and now that she'd found it again, she didn't want to leave it. "You keep my green sweater, okay?" she told Tina.

Tina looked startled. "I don't want—"

"Wear it on the first day of school."

"What if you want to wear it?"

Sarah knew she was going to miss the start of school this year. "Just wear it," Sarah insisted, squeezing Tina's hand with what little strength she had left.

After Sarah had hugged a sobbing Richie, her mother helped her out of bed. As they started for the door, a sense of urgency came over Sarah. There were so many things left undone. She said, "Please, wait. Listen—I don't want the One Last Wish money to go to waste. Make sure it goes to Tina and Richie . . . in case . . ."

"We can discuss that later. Right now, I want to get you out of here," her mother said, holding Sarah firmly around the waist.

Sarah refused to be sidetracked. "The family can use the money, Mom."

"That's thoughtful of you, but you'll be back to spend the money with us."

"Will you just promise me?" Sarah pleaded.

Her mother nodded. "I'll take care of it as soon as possible. Don't look so frantic—Dr. Hernandez will fix you up, and you can help me shop for whatever you want to buy."

"I'm scared," Sarah confessed. "This time, it's different." Whenever she'd gone to the hospital before, it had been for treatments. This time, she was sick, and not from any chemo. She was flushed with fever and felt as if she were melting from the inside. She had been warned that her leukemia was active again. After five years of fighting it, Sarah was battle-weary.

"Don't be frightened. We're family, and we'll be with you all the way. We're going to stop this thing somehow."

There was so much Sarah wanted to do, to say. "I forgot to tell you thank you," she whispered to her mom.

"For what?"

"For putting up with me all summer. For letting me search for my birth mother, even though you didn't want me to."

"Now that it's over and done, I'm glad you did it. I'm glad I was able to meet her for myself."

"Why?"

"Because it took the mystery out of her. It helped me see her as a flesh-and-blood person. I'm grateful to her for giving you up."

Sarah understood. Janelle Warren had done what she'd had to do at the time of Sarah's birth, and Sarah no longer held it against her—or her parents for keeping it from her. "She has a nice life. We're better off without each other," Sarah said.

Her mom squeezed her hand. "All I know, Sarah, is that while I may not have carried you beneath my heart for nine months, I've always carried you *in* my heart. That will never change. You'll live in my heart forever. I love you, Sarah."

"I love you too, Mom." They held one another,

until Sarah, too weak to stand, glanced longingly around her room and said, "I'm ready."

Once her dad settled her in the car, Sarah asked, "Will you bring Tina and Richie to see me this weekend?"

"I couldn't keep them away." He tucked the blanket under her chin, and Sarah saw that his eyes were misty.

"You'll take good care of them, won't you?"

"Yes."

"And Mom, too?"

"And Mom, too. You were my firstborn, Sarah. Don't forget that. I'm so proud of you."

"Although I was grafted onto the McGreggor family tree?" she asked.

"Grafts have a way of turning out an entirely different blossom—unique and special."

"I love you, Daddy."

"I love you, baby."

Numb and feverish, Sarah lay back on the seat while her mom and dad climbed into the front. Tina held Richie, and they gazed anxiously through the car window. Richie clung to Tina, tears smudging his face.

"Hurry home," Tina called as the car backed out of the driveway.

Sarah didn't answer, so certain she was that she'd never see her home again.

Twenty

IN THE HOSPITAL in Memphis, Sarah was immediately placed in an isolation unit. No one came into her room without donning sterile paper gowns, head coverings, and masks. "It's a massive infection," Dr. Hernandez told Sarah and her parents. "And you have no resistance to fight it off."

"What will you do?" Sarah heard her dad ask.

"Keep her isolated, pump her full of antibiotics, and pray that we find a bone marrow donor for her," Dr. Hernandez answered.

For Sarah, time passed, but she couldn't keep track of days and nights. All around her, people came and went dressed in masks and rubber gloves. An IV line was hooked to her arm, and a heart monitor to her chest. She knew her parents took turns staying with her, for she'd wake in the night and see one of them sitting by her bedside. It comforted her, knowing they were within arm's reach.

As some signs of improvement came, Dr. Hernandez warned that the antibiotic treatment was only a stopgap. Although they had stemmed the infection, her white blood count was alarmingly high—her leukemia was active and destructive.

One evening, Dr. Hernandez came rushing into Sarah's room. "You and your mother must see this," she said, still tying on her mask.

She turned on the TV monitor that hung from the wall in the corner of the room. The face of one of the network's evening newscasters filled the screen. Midsentence, he was saying, ". . . final story from Ringgold, Georgia, where a young girl walked into our affiliate station to make this eloquent plea for her sister's life."

Sarah almost choked as Tina's face came onto the monitor. Staring straight into the camera, Tina said, "My sister has leukemia, and if she had a bone marrow transplant, she could probably be cured. But she can't get one because her doctors can't find a compatible donor. It's not that there aren't compatible donors, you see . . . it's just that one hasn't been discovered yet.

"That's because not enough people are willing to become donors. It's real simple to be one. If you're between eighteen and fifty-five and in good health, you can be a donor. And maybe you'll be the one to help Sarah. She's only fifteen. She's too young to die."

The camera zoomed in on a very tight shot of Tina's face. "All you have to do is have a little blood drawn, sign a consent form, and become a part of the National Marrow Donor Program. And someday, if you're lucky, you'll get a call telling you that you're a preliminary match. The doctors do some more blood work on you, and then if you're still a match, they take some of your healthy marrow and transplant it into the person who needs it—like my sister."

Slowly, a big smile spread across Tina's face. "I know lots of people watch this news show every night, so I hope all of you will go to your doctor tomorrow and get your blood checked. Maybe you'll be the person who saves Sarah."

The camera zoomed out, and a reporter recapped the story and added some details. Then she turned to the camera and said, "Thank you, Tina. And good-night, Sarah. God bless."

Dr. Hernandez flipped off the set and came over to Sarah's bed. "That was a gutsy thing for your sister to do," she said. "Totally amazing that she got on national news."

Sarah felt a surge of exhilaration that almost carried her off the bed. "Tina did it for me, Mom," she said. "And millions of people saw it."

Her mother threaded her way through the maze of tubes and wires and hugged Sarah tightly.

"There's more," Dr. Hernandez said. "One of the wire services picked up the story. It's being carried in newspapers all over the country. Just think about it, Sarah, people will read about you, and hundreds will respond. I know they will."

"Maybe one of them will be a match," her mother said.

Dr. Hernandez smiled. "Maybe. The bigger the number of volunteers, the better the odds."

When Tina came that weekend, Sarah held her

and wept, overcome with gratitude. "How did you come up with the idea?" she asked.

"It was a brainstorm I had right after Mom and Dad took you to the hospital," Tina admitted sheepishly. "I told Scott, and he helped me."

"How?"

"He drove me to the TV station, and we talked our way into seeing one of those consumer advocate reporters. She was really nice, and once I told her what we wanted to do—tell people about the donor registry—she did an interview for the local evening news. She called later to say that the people at the network liked the interview so much, they would run it on the evening news for the whole country to see." Tina adjusted her paper mask, and Sarah could tell that behind it, she was grinning. "I'll bet everybody in the country saw me and knows about you by now."

Sarah wondered if her birth mother had seen it, then knew it didn't matter. "Thank you, Tina."

"I hope it helps. The reporter said that it would be nice to run full-page ads in newspapers, or order up billboards in some of the bigger cities. That way, even more people could get the message." She puckered her brow thoughtfully. "It's a good idea, but I know those things cost a lot of money."

Sarah *had* a lot of money. Her eyes grew wide with revelation, and her gaze locked onto her father and mother. Her father read her thoughts instantly and, barely able to contain the excitement in his voice said, "I'll get right on it."

The drama of the moment was lost on Tina, who continued talking. "I also wanted to do it for you because I was feeling kind of guilty about something."

"About what?" Sarah returned her attention to her sister.

"I was glad when you found out you didn't have any other sisters. Even though it meant you couldn't have the bone marrow you needed. That was selfish of me, but I didn't want you to like any sister better than you like me." She peeked over the top of her mask. "Are you mad at me?"

"There's only one of you, Tina. No one could ever take your place." Sarah knew that was true. She saw that even if she had a hundred sisters, Tina would be number one. Of course, they'd had their differences, but they were sisters, bound more tightly than ever. Sarah cleared her throat, afraid she'd break down and cry. "Where's Richie?"

"Still getting all that gear on," Tina said.

Richie came through the double doors in a burst with Dr. Hernandez. The long paper gown trailed behind him, and the mask almost covered his face. He crawled up on a chair beside Sarah's bed and stared down into her face. "I feel like it's Halloween," he said.

Everyone laughed. Looking around at them, Sarah felt so deeply moved, she choked back her emotions. Here, in a hospital ICU room, were the people whom she loved most in the world. Her family was with her—her real family. All the money in the world couldn't buy what she already had—a family who cared for her, loved her, fought for her, worked for her. At that moment, she felt as if her heart would burst with love for them.

"What now?" Sarah asked Dr. Hernandez, who stood at the foot of her bed, looking on.

"Now, we wait," the doctor said, "and we hope that lots of people volunteer to become donors."

Sarah hoped it wouldn't be too long a wait. Waiting could be so tedious. "Do I have to stay in isolation?"

"Yes. You're too vulnerable to infection."

Sarah felt exhaustion creeping over her, and sleep reaching out for her. She gazed up at the cherubic face of her brother. "Sing me a song, Richie. One of your favorites."

His head bobbed in assent, then his little child's voice began chanting, "There was a farmer had a dog, and Bingo was his name-o . . ."

As Richie continued singing, Sarah closed her eyes. "Faith, courage, and hope"—that was what JWC had given her, more than the money. She knew she had so much to be grateful for, no matter what happened tomorrow.

ABOUT THE AUTHOR

LURLENE MCDANIEL has been a professional writer for more than twenty years and has written radio and television scripts, promotional and advertising copy, and a magazine column. She began writing inspirational novels about life-altering situations for children and young adults after one of her sons was diagnosed with juvenile diabetes. She lives in Chattanooga, Tennessee.

Lurlene McDaniel's popular Bantam Starfire books include: *Too Young to Die, Goodbye Doesn't Mean Forever, Somewhere Between Life and Death, Time to Let Go, When Happily Ever After Ends,* and the other One Last Wish novels *A Time to Die* and *Mourning Song.*

A NEW BOOK EVERY OTHER MONTH

ONE LAST WISH

*Moving new books about young
people faced with the end of life—
just as their lives are beginning, by
Lurlene McDaniel*

☐ A TIME TO DIE   29809-7
$3.50/$3.99 in Canada

☐ MOURNING SONG   29810-0
$3.50/$3.99 in Canada

☐ MOTHER, HELP ME LIVE   29811-9
$3.50/$3.99 in Canada

☐ SOMEONE LIVES, SOMEONE DIES   29842-9
$3.50/$3.99 In Canada

☐ SIXTEEN AND DYING   29932-8
$3.50/$3.99 In Canada

☐ LET HIM LIVE   56067-0
$3.50/$3.99 in Canada

**Bantam Books, Dept DA 45, 2451 South Wolf Road,
Des Plaines, IL 60018**
Please send me the items I have checked above. I am
enclosing $ ____ (please add $2.50 to cover postage and
handling). Send check or money order, no cash or
C.O.D's please.
Mr/Mrs _____
Address_____
City/State_____ Zip_____
Please allow four to six weeks for delivery.   DA 45 -2/93
Prices and availability subject to change without notice.

STARFIRE

Ten-Hankie Reading from
Lurlene McDaniel

☐ 28008-2 **TOO YOUNG TO DIE** $3.50

☐ 28007-4 **GOODBYE DOESN'T
           MEAN FOREVER** $2.95

☐ 28349-9 **SOMEWHERE BETWEEN
           LIFE AND DEATH** $3.50

☐ 28350-2 **TIME TO LET GO** $3.50

☐ 28897-0 **NOW I LAY ME DOWN
           TO SLEEP** $3.50

Bantam Books, Dept. DA38, 2451 South Wolf Road, Des Plaines, IL 60018

Please send me the items I have checked above. I am enclosing $_____
(please add $2.50 to cover postage and handling). Send check or money
order, no cash or C.O.D.s please.

Mr/Ms _____

Address _____

City/State _____ Zip _____

DA38–11/92

Please allow four to six weeks for delivery.